MW01136916

THE DEACON

FIRST IN A NEW SERIES

OF

FRONTIER WESTERNS

DOUG BALL

OTHER BOOKS BY
DOUG BALL

Tales of The Old West
Blood on the Zuni

Vengeance

Lone Tree

Tales of The Not So Old West
Gentle Rebellion

4 X Armed

Rebellion's New Beginnings

The State of Arizona Series
Alternative Current History

State of Defense (also in audiobook)

State of Threat (also in audiobook)

State of Peril (also in audiobook

The Silent Service
Sailor

Biblical Studies
Puzzling Theology

The Fishy Prophet

What Ought to Be

Called to Good Works

Copyright 2016 – Douglas H. Ball

Cover design by the Author
Cover art Shutterstock

This is a work of fiction. Any resemblance between characters and persons living or dead is purely coincidental.

This book is dedicated to
Zane Richardson
who mentored me as a
teacher of the Word

And of course
Patti

The DEACON

1

"Boy, it's all about the money. Never forget that. It's all about the money. Now get out there on the road and bang that drum. We need the money they'll bring to the show. You also need to remember that it's all a show, once you get serious with this stuff you are in trouble with a capital T."

I shuffled out of the huge blue and white tent carrying a bass drum that was almost as big around as I was tall. At twelve years old, I knew the routine well. I was to bang the drum while standing next to the sign that said, "Revival. Come for a fresh anointing of the power of God." I was to look cute and smile as wagons and horses loaded with people went past on their way to the homes and businesses of the community where my father had set up the tent this time.

The routine was always the same. I'd bang the drum and my father would preach. My father's current entertainment was a woman he'd picked up from a saloon about three months past who sang sweet enough, but dealt with life with a foul mouth and even worse heart. But, she was pretty, could sing, and dressed like the pious proper lady, which she wasn't, for the meetings. After the preacher and psalm singing were over, she and my father would retire to the caravan wagon to drink themselves to sleep.

I, on the other hand, would lie awake half the night listening to their foul conversation and plans for the money that had filled the offering plate. My biggest hope was that this was one of those rare occasions when my father would toss me a silver dollar and say, "Run into town, son, and buy yourself a treat." That hadn't happened in quite awhile.

The offerings were down.

A kid about my own age stopped and asked, "Can I hit that thing a couple of times?"

"Sure." I moved back from the drum and its stand and handed the new kid the stick with the round ball of soft felt wrapped around the end. "Don't hit it too hard, you might break the skin and I'd get a whooping, a bad whooping."

"Okay." The new kid took the stick and gave the drum three healthy whacks causing the drum to tip.

I grabbed the drum, "Not quite that hard and hold the edge of the drum like this when you hit it." I showed the kid how to hold it by the tightening rod across the top side.

The kid grabbed the rod and hit the drum a couple more times. "This is fun. Do they pay you for this job?"

"Nah. My dad's the preacher."

"The one that was preaching in the saloon last night?"

"That would be him."

"Never heard of a preacher that got drunk and preached for free."

"He weren't preaching for free. He was preaching so's them bums would hear the Word and repent from their sinful ways and buy him a drink."

The kid shook his head as he continued to beat the drum, "Sounds fishy to me. My Ma said that a preacher should never allow foul alcohol to touch his lips."

"I doubt if the booze ever touches his lips, he slugs them down so fast. His tongue maybe, but not his lips."

"I'll have to check with Ma on that." He smiled at the thought of being able to counter his mother's words.

"Come on by tonight and I'll get you a seat up front. Sometimes Pa gets to preaching so loud and frantic, he spits on the folks in the front couple of rows. Especially if he's got a snoot full."

"I don't want no one spittin' on me. Ma says spit carries diseases and stuff."

"Okay, you can sit on the side of the stage near the piano with me."

"I could do that. Gee, thanks."

"My name's Daniel, what's yours?"

"Michael. Just like the Archangel."

"I'm named after some buckaroo that herded lions."

"He must have been one tough hand."

"He was. The King made him his right hand man."

Two cowboys rode by laughing at the boys beating the drum. "Ben, we gonna come back and hurrah this tent tonight?"

"Sounds like a great idea. I ain't heard a hell fire and damnation preacher in at least five years. Might be a good time. If he ain't lively enough, we can help him by kickin' up the action."

I heard the conversation and told myself to remember to tell my father.

I didn't.

That evening Michael showed up just as the 'singer' was belting out "Bringing in the Sheaves." The crowd grew to fill about half the tent and its 70 folding chairs. There were about a dozen cowboys standing in the back with bottles of various varieties of booze from beer to rotgut being flaunted. All of them were commenting and gesturing with volume and vigor.

I remembered the two cowboys riding by and ran to my father. "Dad, the cowboys are planning to hurrah you and the service tonight."

"Don't you worry, son, the Good Lord is in charge here tonight as He is every night," he said as he laughed at his own words, which he did a lot.

"Dad, I don't really think it's right laughing at something like that."

"You're right, son, but few there are that realize that, and I am one of them." He walked to the podium, laid out his Bible and notes, and then hit the bass drum standing in its stand there beside him with a couple of good licks just as the demure dancehall girl finished her song.

"Thank you, Evelyn, for that enlightening Word of God in song. Let's all give Evelyn a rousing hand of appreciation."

The audience gave a half-hearted response. The cowboys in the back were cheering like mad. One of them even called out, "That ain't no Evelyn, that's Miss Daisy from Wichita. I saw her there last year when I hauled beef into that burg."

The audience laughed louder at that than the response was to the song.

"Let us pray," said the preacher.

Two hours later after the bucket had been passed around three times, the Preacher gave an impassioned altar call for, "All you sinners need to repent and come to the feet of Jesus. Now is the day of repentance, not tomorrow. Come, come one and come all. Now is the light of Jesus shining brightest in the eyes of your heart. Come and live forevermore with Him in Paradise just as the thief on the cross. Come and enjoy the benefits of His Salvation. No more problems. No more worries. He heals, come and be healed. Come now. We will sing that great hymn of the faith, 'The Old Rugged Cross.' Miss Evelyn will lead us."

Miss Evelyn stood and sang with a dozen tears in her voice.

The crowd split. One group just remained seated. The other 15 or so got up and walked the aisle to the front and were greeted by the Right Reverend Doctor Lawrence P. Fount, Larry Fount on his arrest records. The head Deacon of the local Presbyterian Church asked Dr. Fount, "May I assist you, Sir?"

"Why certainly, young man." He could see his backwards collar and knew this man would appreciate the increase in his own flock.

Some folks hit their knees and begged for the forgiveness of their sins, others cried out for healing, the rest of those up front just stood waiting for whatever was supposed to happen. All except for one old cowboy. That one old cowboy began the journey to the front and passed out cold to end up flat on his face in the middle of the crowd. He got stepped on a few times, but never felt it. He would do his feeling in the morning.

The Reverend Fount screamed at the top of his lungs, "This man is so overwhelmed with the power of God that he has passed out at the relieving of the burden of all his sins. Let's shout hallelujah in praise."

"He passed out drunk," yelled a cowboy from the rear of the tent.

The seated crowd laughed and catcalled concerning the issue.

"He's a boozer and a loozer."

"That old reprobate."

"Somebody dowse him with a bucket of water."

Just as the fun was rippling through the tent, the old cowboy got up, drew his six shooter, and proceeded to put five holes in the roof of the big top. The crowd hit the floor as if they were all struck by the power of God. The old cowboy staggered to the back and exited through the door of the tent.

The Reverend Fount said, "Damn, more holes to patch before they run."

He left the tent as Evelyn sang the first verse, the only one she knew, again for the fifth time.

By the time she finished the first verse again, the crowd was well thinned, I was left to put out the lamps and lanterns hanging here and there, along with buttoning up the tent door. I noticed the Reverend

Father, my Father, had not forgotten the offering which had resided in a tin bucket near the entrance.

"Must have been skimpy, he left the bucket." I went to my blanket under the caravan.

2

A month and ten towns later, the tent sat in the dirt at the end of the main business section of Las Vegas, New Mexico. The wind blew as the six hired men struggled to get the tent erected until the Reverend Fount called an end to the struggle and just had me set up the chairs. The weather being pleasant and the location at the crest of a slight rise said much for the outdoor, no tent set up. No one would be cold and due to the breeze, the mosquitoes would not bother the folks. There was even a convenient rock, flat on top and large enough to be the stage. The piano would not fit, nor could it be lifted up to those heights, but a simple four step ladder sufficed to allow the Reverend and Miss Evelyn an easy and modest assent to the God given platform.

With the easy site setup allowing the Reverend plenty of time before the show, he descended into the community to share the joy he felt with the folks of said community. There being five separate buildings which merchandised the nectars he sought gave him ample opportunity to spread the good word around concerning the Joy that would be available on the hilltop that evening.

Unfortunately, he spent more time imbibing in the merchandise than he did spreading the good news of joy. Come the advertised time of 6 PM, he was only semi-conscious in the caravan. No efforts of Miss Evelyn could arouse him fully. Finally, I went in as Miss Evelyn took the stage to keep the masses occupied until I could wake up the Preacher.

After three verses of 'We Shall Gather at the River,' I got fed up and threw a bucket of water on in the Preacher's face. Of course that was not a good thing to do since it doused all the man's clothing from the waist up and left the bed a sodden mess. The Reverend sputtered and cursed like a sailor until he gave out with the best idea he ever had, "You go preach to them, Daniel. Tell them how God delivered your namesake from the Lions."

"I can't preach. You're the preacher, not me. What do I know about preaching?"

"It's all about the money, son. Put on the show and they will drop their last penny in that tin bucket. It is all about the money." He fell back, out cold.

I grabbed a good shirt and coat from the bottom drawer, climbed into them, and ran for the stairs to the platform. Arriving at the top I found I could not see over the podium, so it was tossed aside with a crash that brought all attention to the front. Evelyn ended her song at the same moment.

"Ladies and Gentlemen, my earthly father is ill." A long period of laughter from the audience followed. "He has anointed me to speak to you tonight. If you are disappointed, you may leave and with this set up you may leave in any direction you wish." Again laughter.

"My name is Daniel. It comes from a man of ancient Israel in captivity. He was a slave to the highest man in the world of that day." I went on to finish the story.

"As Daniel was saved from the lions and promoted to the highest position under the king, you, yes you, can be promoted to the highest position under God by using the same faith Daniel used in his stand against the evil advisors of the king. This old world will tell you that you are alright, but God says you must have faith in His Son, Jesus, to be all right. You cannot be half right and be in the presence of God, you cannot even be mostly right to be in the presence of God. You must be ALL RIGHT, and that only happens when you totally give in to the desires of God and let Him lead you to your resurrection one day."

Miss Evelyn fell to her knees as she sang her rendition of 'The Old Rugged Cross' again and again. Tears rolled down her cheeks. Between lines she cried out, "Save me, Jesus." Everyone thought it was part of the show. Miss Daisy (Evelyn) meant it from the bottom of her heart. As she began the first verse again, she raised her head and cried, "I repent. I will be your child. Bring on the lions."

I knelt beside her, "Don't you think you are overdoing it a bit?"

"I am not acting. This is real. I have never felt like this. The happiness in my heart is smothering the pain of my life history. Oh, the joy." She started the first verse again.

I looked at the reactions of the crowd and wondered what was going on. This had never happened when my father preached. Even the cowboys from the back of the room were up front on their knees. Many of the crowd were crying, many were just sitting in their chairs with lips twitching. One man was flat on his face sobbing.

Folks had walked the aisle for my father, but never this proportion of the crowd, and never with such sincerity. There were only three left in their chairs showing no reaction. I was scared and walked back to the caravan not knowing what else to do.

My father called out, "Did you do it?"

"Yes, Dad. I don't understand the reaction."

"What? Did they boo you or throw things at you?"

"No. They got all emotional and cried a lot."

The man got out of his bed, stumbling over his shoes, and walked to the platform. The sight was one he had never seen before. Evelyn was on her knees confessing every single sin she could remember, the crowd was still on site in various positions of surrender, and even the cowboys were quiet, not mocking any of it.

"What did that boy do?" he whispered as he walked in sock covered feet through the crowd.

3

The next night the crowd began to form on the hilltop more than an hour early. There was even some jostling for the prime seats down front. Two cowboys got in a fight over a chair that was the last one on the back row. Miss Evelyn was dressed and mingling with the crowd a half hour before the show was to start.

"Oh, yes, you will be amazed at what God can do with your life once you surrender to Him through Jesus, the Christ. It is such a powerful moment and it lasts for the rest of eternity," Miss Evelyn told one young painted dance hall gal on the front row.

"I hope he's done before my boss misses me at the Cowboy Corral. I'm one of his biggest attractions and he won't treat me nice if I ain't there when the boys hit town, it being Friday and all."

"I know whereof you speak, gal. I was in your shoes not 24 hours ago. Now I belong to Jesus and no man is gonna make me do anything I don't wanna do no more."

"Oh, that sounds so sweet. Tell me more at the end. You can walk me back, can't you?"

"Maybe. It depends on the response."

"Response to what."

"The Word of God. That boy delivers it like no one I ever heard before."

In the caravan, the boy, me, was being shoved into his clean, second best shirt. "You just go out there and tell them another Bible story like you did last night. How about the ten lepers? Remember? Jesus healed ten lepers and only one came back to say, 'thanks.' The rest went on their merry way without ever givin' a hoot who it was that healed them."

"But Dad, I ain't never been to no Bible school like you. I ain't a preacher."

"That crowd last night said differently, Daniel. They ate it up. The offering was one of the biggest we've ever had. It's all about the money, boy, all about the money. You get out there and wow them with another story. You can do it. About time I retired anyhow. Too many towns know me."

"I'll do'er one more time. Then that's it," I looked him in the eye, "I hope."

"Give them heaven and they'll fill the bucket."

"I'm a phony, Dad. I don't believe any of this stuff. It's all hooey or so you been telling me for all my life."

"They believe it and they are the ones that fill the bucket."

"One more time," I said, leaving the caravan for the rock platform.

The crowd saw me coming just as I saw the crowd. Every seat was filled with a person whose eyes were on me and I weren't too excited about that, either. The crowd went totally silent.

Miss Evelyn looked up to see why and then moved to her position on the rock. She looked at me and smiled. After all, I had shown her the way to a new life. She began to sing a new song she had never sung for anyone before. She had heard it as a child in New Hampshire when her folks would drag her, practically kicking and screaming, to the Congregational Church just outside of town. She sang, 'What a Friend We Have in Jesus.' She didn't plan it, it just came. The words flowed through her mind and out her mouth, verse after verse, until she was finished.

I stood on the platform in awe of the beauty we, the crowd and me, had just heard. The crowd sat or stood in silence, most with their mouths wide open as if to catch all the music. One cowboy sitting on his horse way off to one side, took off his hat and hung it on the horn of his saddle and started clapping. The crowd slowly and reverently joined in as they stood before the crying Miss Evelyn.

Miss Evelyn yelled through her tears, "It's all true. You can have a friend in Jesus."

The clapping got louder.

The cowboy ground reined his horse and walked slowly to the front of the rock platform and sat down in the dirt. I raised both hands as I had seen my Dad do to get the crowd's attention. They just kept clapping for Miss Evelyn. I let them.

She bowed and raised her hands. The crowd went silent. "Thank you. That was a song I learned a long time ago against my will, but today I sang it from my heart in His will. Please listen to what Daniel has to say to you." The crowd shifted their eyes to look at the twelve year old boy in a boiled shirt and scuffed shoes.

I stepped closer to the edge of the stone platform.

An hour later I finished with, "Most of you want to be able to see, but few of you will come to Jesus for healing. He, and He alone can open your eyes to the sin in your lives that requires you to repent in order to truly know Jesus as the Savior. Then there will be even fewer that will come to the front and truly repent in faith before the throne of God that this rock symbolizes. Come won't you?" I looked down, "Cowboy, you're gonna have to move."

The cowboy moved. He crawled to the rock, put one hand on his face and the other on the rock, before he yelled, "Jesus, heal me."

Miss Evelyn scurried to the back of the rock, down the ladder, and around to the cowboy. She kneeled beside him, "Cry out to God and tell him how sorry you are that your sins required Jesus to go to the cross and be the blood sacrifice for your sins."

The cowboy cried. He cried so loud his friends came up to see what was going on. By the time they arrived, the area between the chairs and the rock was filled with people in tears and on their knees before this God that I had presented to them. Miss Evelyn went from person to person talking, comforting, and testifying of the Grace of God in her life. She even yelled at one point, "Yesterday I was in darkness, but since I met Jesus last night, I am in the light. I am free. I am free. I am free at last."

The young saloon girl she had talked to before the service caught her, "Tell me how I can hide from my boss and live with Jesus."

I carried the bucket to the back of the area where most of the folks had entered. As I walked folks tossed bills and change into the bucket. The bucket got heavier as I approached the spot where it belonged and sat the bucket on a rock that stood about two feet tall and placed a small sign on a stick in it that read, "Donations accepted," and walked toward the caravan.

Person after person grabbed me and asked me to pray. I prayed. I didn't believe it would do an ounce of good, but I prayed. I must have prayed a dozen times before I could break through the crowd and was able to reach the caravan. The clutching hands of the crowd fell away as I shrugged my way through the last ones and into the clear behind the rock platform.

"Dad," I said as I entered the caravan, "You just aren't gonna believe what I saw tonight."

My father wasn't there. He was in a local saloon, fondling a dancehall gal and drinking all the unguarded booze left behind the bar.

The gal didn't mind. He had money and was free with it.

Miss Evelyn reached the last person face down on the dirt to find the cowboy. He was crying and shouting his sins as he begged for forgiveness. Miss Evelyn said, "Cowboy, that Bible says that if we repent and ask God for forgiveness, He will forgive. That's a promise He keeps on a daily basis in your life."

"Miss Evelyn, I needed tonight. I knew I was living wrong and now I'm dealing with it thanks to you and that boy, that preacher. Jesus is my friend just like you sang at the beginning. Where's the boy?"

"He left." She knew I didn't believe what I told these folks, but she knew that God would forgive me one day when I did repent and follow the Word I was teaching. I surely didn't believe it as I preached it.

4

Three years later I stood on the platform in the largest venue in Denver and looked out over several hundred people of all ages, creeds, and colors. The message was one of a thief that was dying from the nails in his hands and feet that held him to a cross piece of rough sawn timber. The thief was hanging on a cross next to the dying Jesus. The thief admitted he was guilty of his deeds and deserved to die, and told the world from his cross that Jesus had done nothing wrong. He was hanging there for no reason other than the jealousy of the priesthood of the church of his day. He was hanging there in reality because that's where His Father wanted him. He was hanging there to pay the penalty before God for all the sins of a lost world.

As I taught that last sentence something happened in the heart of a 15 year old young sinner standing on a platform in front of thousands of people. Somehow I became totally convinced that all I had been teaching for three years was really true and that this same Jesus died for me, too. I knew that the bucket was sitting at the back of the room with its small sign. I knew it was overflowing with the donations of all these people. I knew that it wasn't all about the money.

IT WAS ALL ABOUT JESUS.

I BELIEVED IT ALL!

I fell to my knees and cried, "Father, forgive me, a sinner," and fainted in tears.

The next morning just before noon the Denver Tribune put out a special edition with black headlines reading, "BOY PREACHER FALLS FOR HIS OWN MESSAGE" in three lines above the fold. The article read:

> *Last night at the Miner's Hall, 15 year old Daniel Fount came to the fount of Jesus in the middle of his own sermon. The young preacher, son of the infamous Right Reverend Lawrence P. Fount, was approximately half way through his usual sermon time when he swooned on stage.*
>
> *Miss Evelyn, the singer with the preacher, says he has been working excessive hours with new believers in Jesus and was totally exhausted. His father, the Right Reverend, stated that he didn't know what happened until this morning. Rumor had it that the father was in the notorious Bucket of Blood Saloon with one, Big Bottom Kate, on his lap for most of the evening throwing money around like it was confetti thrown at a political parade.*

Dr. Elmont Goode, a physician, is reported to have said that he could find no reason for the young preacher's nose dive to the stage. The good Doctor Goode repaired the man's broken nose and received a $10 bill for his services.

Young Preacher Daniel Fount stated to this reporter that the Revival will continue tonight a 7 PM at the Miner's Hall where he will explain everything. A hearty crowd is expected.

Miss Evelyn will sing.

At five minutes to 7 PM that evening, back stage in the Miner's Hall I looked at Evelyn, "Evelyn, I need you to sing like you have only sung once before and that was the night in Las Vegas when you sang 'What a Friend We Have in Jesus.' I want you to sing it just like you did that night."

I turned, "Dad, I want you well out of here. It could get dangerous. There were three notes delivered this afternoon concerning the phoniness of our ministry and the use of the funds donated by the audience. I may get hurt, but there is no sense anyone else getting hurt. Evelyn, you leave by the side door as soon as I begin to speak."

Dad went out the back door with a smile.

Miss Evelyn said, "I won't do that, Dan. I will be in the wings praying."

"There is no reason for God to protect us tonight. I have sinned greatly and you have allowed it to happen even after you became a believer. So, go."

"No!"

I gave up, "Thank you. I'll need all the prayer I can get. But, if it starts getting violent, you run."

"Lady don't run too well dressed like this. I'll be there praying." She pointed to the left wing.

The stage hand that was still working with them came by and said, "Ten minutes, Preacher Fount. Miss Evelyn, the piano player asked if you would begin with a couple of songs starting now. The crowd is sounding rowdy and angry."

"On my way. Pray for me, Dan."

The stagehand said, "She's gonna need it. I saw lots of rotten vegetables and fruit out there as I watched the front door. There was also a basket of eggs. Not a single person has dropped a penny in the bucket." He paused as if he were looking for the right words to say. "I know how you feel, but remember – the Truth shall set you free, and Jesus is the Truth. I'll be praying with Miss Evelyn."

"Thank you. Stay away from me if it gets bad."

"Don't worry. I got a wife and three kids to think of. I'll drop the curtain if you say so."

"I won't."

The sweet sounds of Miss Evelyn's singing drifted through the curtains and reached my ears bringing me to a peace as I prayed which brought me to total comfort in the midst of this turmoil. I checked the backstage clock. Six minutes until I would walk out there and put everything on the line for the cause of Jesus, this time, the first time in truth.

I walked to the edge of the down-left curtain and peeked through the footlights illuminating Miss Evelyn at the down-right stage corner as she sang, 'What a Friend We Have in Jesus' with her clear, carrying voice. The audience stirred like an ant bed a horse had just stomped on.

She finished.

I walked on stage to center front, three feet behind the center footlight.

5

"Ladies and gentlemen, brothers and sisters, I stand here before you a humbled man. As many of you may have seen last night, I was struck down by the power of knowing that I was a sinner and needed the Christ I have been preaching. My father was a fraud and I have been a fraud for just over 3 years. Now I am the new man I have spoken of many times. Now, I am one transformed to being God's man by His power. I stand before you a true, renewed man of God, convicted of the truth of the words I have been preaching by the Holy Spirit, and ready to share those same words with you in truth and power."

A slow rumble came from the crowd. It sounded like the lions were being turned loose and hungry. The first egg caught me up side of the head followed by a downpour of rotten vegetables and more eggs. I stood there as if to say to them, 'I deserve what you are doing and much more.'

The audience yelled and screamed. A couple cowboys came up to the stage and dropped a loop over my head before dragging me off, down the center aisle, and into the street where they took dallies on their saddle horns and drug me from the hall to the edge of town, about a mile. Fortunately, the road was fairly soft dirt with few rocks. At the edge of town, they turned me loose.

More vegetables hit me and a couple of eggs. I stood, looking at the rags that covered my nakedness. It was a long, loud walk back to the venue with angry folks pushing and shoving all the way. Miss Evelyn walked beside me getting hit with vegetables and one egg. The stage hand met us at the door with a shotgun carried across his chest.

He calmly said, "You folks go home. Shows over for tonight," and calmly shut the door in their faces.

The next night twenty three people came and sat at the back. None of them said a word or made a noise as I followed Miss Evelyn on to the stage. They said and did nothing during my hour of preaching. When I was done they got up and left, and that was the end of that.

The third night the place was packed again. The vegetables and eggs were back. My skin itched and scabs cracked as I climbed the stairs from the back door to the stage level. My sermon was imbedded in my mind.

When I finally took the stage and gave the apology again for the third time, the audience sat or stood in silence. Miss Evelyn began signing softly to my right. The crowd slowly gathered in the words of the song, 'Just as I Am,' they stood and joined in the singing. Not one verse was missed. Not one person stood silent, they hummed if they did not know the words

I stood in genuine humility with head hanging and hands clasped at my chest in awe of the power of the truth.

The first rotten thing hit me, a potato. The rancid stench filled my nose as the eggs and garbage pelted me harder and harder until I was covered in the slime of an angry city. I fell to my knees crying from the sense that I deserved all this and they had every right to vent on me.

Evelyn sang louder as she joined me on the stage. She became the target as she joined me on her knees. Words like hypocrite and liar filled the air. The venom of the words was stunning to my young mind. How could they hate so much that another had joined the Kingdom of God? How?

Louder and louder the audience raged until all became silence as if someone turned off the entire group at once.

I looked up. All I could see were the backs of folks leaving the building. They were done. I felt that I had only begun. Tomorrow night I would be here with the power of the message, the Gospel of Jesus, and not the sweetness of a man trying to lure the dollars from the suckered crowd.

There was no time to mourn or pout, no time to second guess, I had to preach. All that I was told me that. "This is our baptism, Evelyn. Let's get to work."

There was no reply.

I looked to the right and saw Evelyn lying on the stage, blood coming from her forehead.

"Oh, God, please let her live," I cried louder than i had ever spoken before.

"You care that much?" Evelyn asked.

"Yes," I replied, startled. "You are the only mother I have ever really known."

"Let's get this mess cleaned up. We got a service tomorrow night that will be a world changer, I'm sure." My face was bright red and it wasn't from exertion.

The cleanup took until the small hours of the morning. The stage hand had left around midnight leaving only Evelyn and me. I was peeled down to shirtsleeves and trousers. Evelyn worked in the dress she started in. "It's destroyed anyhow. The stains and the stink will never come out. I'll trash it when we're done."

As we left the building, rolling the last two wheelbarrows full of garbage, Evelyn started singing, 'More About Jesus Would I Know.'

"Where'd that song come from?"

"It's a new one, I just got the music on. I kinda like it. How about you?"

"It fits, somehow. I like it."

We arrived at the caravan with both of us singing the song. As the song ended again, "Goodnight, Dan."

"Goodnight, Evelyn."

An hour later my father came under the caravan to join me. "She won't open the door, Daniel. Make her open the door."

"No, Dad." I reached up and grabbed a blanket from a shelf dad had built there years ago. "Here. Evelyn and I are living a new life now. You can join us in Jesus, stay with us as my father, or leave. Goodnight." I rolled over as a very drunk and perplexed man tried to figure out what was happening and how to wrap himself in the blanket.

Noon found me walking around town in work clothes hanging new posters all over. The posters read, "The message is the same, but the heart delivering it is changed forever" at the top of the same old poster they had used for years. "Come hear the truth" was at the bottom.

When I finished I stepped into The Grub House to get something to eat only to be received with, "Boo, go away you phony." A cry of "The imposter has arrived, give him an egg," followed. The waitress walked up to me and said, "How could you fake your sermons so well. Only the devil himself would be able to do that."

I replied, "The devil was truly at work." I handed her one of two posters in my hand. "Come see the real thing tonight."

She turned her back and refused the poster.

A large man smelling of blood stepped up to me, "You better get outta town, faker. Most folks don't care much for swindles and you been pulling a swindle. You get on that stage tonight and you are just likely to get tarred and feathered before we lift you high on a splintery rail and carry you out of town."

"I wouldn't try that if I were you." I turned and walked out, head hanging.

Seven rolled around. I watched the seats in the Miner's Hall. Only two were filled. No one was coming. I had purposefully taken the offering bucket and stashed it in the caravan so folks could see I wasn't after the money.

I nodded to Evelyn telling her to step out and start singing. She did. 'Amazing Grace' rang through the hall like it was being sung by an angel. Her new dress sparkled in the light of the candles and lanterns as if it were a piece of the dark summer sky.

The two drunks in the seats were shocked into wakefulness. The first said, "What's that caterwauling, Roger."

Roger replied, "Some cow's got her teat in a ringer and the farmer's still trying to get more milk."

The two of them laughed themselves silly and went back to sleep by the time Miss Evelyn got to the part about ten thousand days.

She finished her two songs and walked off the stage. "Daniel, we're done."

"Meet me on the hill behind the caravan in twenty minutes."

"I can do that."

"Wear old clothes."

"I can do that, too."

I turned and walked to the two drunks, woke them up, and escorted them out of the building so the stagehand could lock up.

The stagehand asked as he ushered me out the stage door, "You done?"

"The hall is paid for the rest of the week. I will use it for the rest of the week and maybe, just maybe, if the Lord is generous, I will pay up on the option for another two weeks."

"Works for me. I gotta be here no matter how it's used or it ain't. No matter to me. I would like to hear more of what you was talkin' of that night before you fainted."

"I'll be here at noon and discuss it with you."

"Where ya off to, Daniel?" the stagehand asked.

"Up yonder hill to pray. Evelyn and I will be up there for quite a spell, I would imagine. I got a lot to confess and get off my chest, and then there's a lot I think needs to happen in this town and I aim to find out if God agrees." I turned to walk away.

"Can anybody come up there, Preacher?"

"You?"

"Yeah. And my wife. She thinks you're a great preacher and a very brave man."

That had me flustered, "Nothing great about me. I just let God go to work on and through me. Come on up and bring a friend or two. I don't care."

"See ya in about an hour. Gotta finish locking up, making sure all the lights are out, and the till is in the safe. Ooops, no till, no safe needed. I just might take ya up on the friend or two."

Setting my face toward the hill, I started walking, dropping my coat off at the caravan, and grabbing a heavier jacked to kneel on and use if it got chilly. The hilltop was empty when I arrived, but the sound of small rocks being disturbed came from behind and I knew at least one other person would be there, Evelyn.

"I'm here," she said.

I fell to my knees and began praying silently with my face raised to the heavens. Evelyn understood and kneeled five feet away. Within minutes we were both on our faces with tears dripping into the dirt. Neither of us heard the stage hand and his wife join the small group. Twenty minutes later six others joined. The Presbyterian preacher brought a few with him a few minutes later.

By 10 PM a crowd of over a hundred was on that hilltop praying, yet not a sound was heard except sobbing.

6

By midnight folks were leaving the hilltop, many of them totally wrung out before their God. At the sound of the city clock announcing 1 AM, the crowd was half diminished. As the sun rose in the east, only two were still there. Each of us was standing with arms outraised welcoming the new day, praying harder that it would be a new day and life for many in the city below them.

I looked at Evelyn, "Let's go eat."

Evelyn replied, "I feel filled."

"So do I, but I am still hungry for food."

We walked down the hill and across the streets until we arrived at The Grub House. No one said a word except the waitress. "What can I getcha this morning, Preacher?"

"Coffee." I looked at Evelyn, who nodded, "Make that two."

"Hey, Jim. Two cups a wide-awake for the Preacher and the Singer."

"Comin' right up."

The waitress handed them a copy of their morning menu which offered eggs, side meat, steak, taters, beans, and grits in any combination cooked any way the cook cooked them.

We both knew what the place had, Evelyn said, "Load a plate for me."

"Same here," I said.

We chose an empty table, sat, and just looked at each other. Two smiles began to grow until I said, "God's gonna do something in the hall tonight that will determine the rest of my life. I really feel like He told me that up on the hill."

"That goes along with what I felt. I feel He told me that my work was just beginning. The other side of that is He wants me to dump your father and stay with you as your opener."

"Dad isn't going to like that after these past years."

"I can no longer live in sin with a man not my husband. He refused to marry me last time I asked him. He was drunk enough to give a bar gal a twenty dollar bill, but not drunk enough to marry an ex-saloon gal and singer. I'm done with him. God said it had to be. I felt I had to sleep with him or I wouldn't have a home or a job. My own stinkin' thinkin' kept me there. Your dad even preached that sermon one time in a camp where folks were all livin' together without benefit of marriage because a preacher had never come to town and he found out. In his case it had nothing to do with sin. He wanted the money they'd pay for the weddings. It worked. He did 22 weddings that afternoon and the least he received was a five dollar nugget which I still have in my case. It's been my mad money for almost six years now. Well, I'm mad but I ain't the one that's gonna be movin' out. I may have been a saloon gal, but I am not one now."

"Sounds good to me." I looked at her with new insight into the complexity of life as a Christian for a woman with a history.

The food arrived and disappeared down our throats faster than a chicken will suck up a worm. I stood, yawned, and stretched, "I'm for a nap. Let's go move Dad out of the caravan. If he ain't there, all the better."

"He's still your earthly father, Dan."

"Yup, he is. He can move underneath with me. Plenty of room for two separate bedrooms under there."

"He isn't gonna like it."

"That is really his problem. He passed the baton to me when he got so drunk he couldn't preach. Now it's my show and he's welcome to tag along."

7

The two of us stood behind Miner's Hall praying. The air was still and sticky telling Denver it was in store for a storm. "Let's get inside before we get soaked."

Evelyn answered, "I really don't want to go in there. There are many ways for God to provide the answers to those prayers on the hilltop." She stopped and stared at the wall for moment or two, "Daniel, where'd all them folks up on that hill come from. Who told them we'd be up there?"

"We'll never know what God is gonna do until the curtain opens and I ain't got the foggiest idea where them folks come from unless the stagehand and his wife invited them."

We entered after knocking on the stage door to get the stage hand to open it.

He smiled, "I'm whipped. I never knew prayer could be such hard work. I joined Jesus last night after my wife explained some of it to me. I still need that conversation we were gonna have."

"Congratulations. I forgot with all the excitement of the hilltop experience. Where'd all them people come from?" I motioned toward the hall, "How's it look?"

"Don't know. I only told the Presbyterian preacher as I passed him on the street." He poked a thumb over his shoulder and said, "I'll find out with you when we draw the curtain. It's very quiet out there and there's just five minutes until start up."

We moved to the rope that controlled the curtain. The piano began quietly. No other noise could be heard. A quiet piano version of 'Amazing Grace' lifted.

Evelyn walked to the middle of the stage still behind the curtain. As the piano got to the closing line of the verse and played the first three sections of the last line, she stepped through the gap onto the stage, down center, to the brightest stage light lifting from the biggest foot light, and began to sing as the piano continued.

Backstage, I could hear no sound from an audience.

I listened as she sang. At the end of the first verse I stepped through the curtain. Every seat was filled. The side aisles and the back were filled with standing men and women. An occasional child could be seen, but all was quiet.

I stood in awe. My body began to shake from fear. Only organized angry people could stay that quiet as they waited for the key word that would loose the lions on the two of us.

I looked out over that crowd with my Bible in hand. They had come and by all that was Holy they would hear the word. I opened the Bible and began to read. "For God so loved, HE LOVES YOU, the world that He gave His only begotten Son, that whosoever, WHOSOEVER, believes on Him, THE SON, should not perish, DIE, BUT, BUT, hear me, BUT have EVERLASTING life. Complete life. No wondering. Tears of joy. No more emptiness. No fear of death. The perfect life for all eternity, THAT MEANS FOREVER. From right now until FOREVER, which never ends.

I nodded to Miss Evelyn telling her it was time to quit the song. Evelyn shook her head and sang louder. I lifted my arms high in a gathering motion, "Come, come as I did a few nights ago. Come to Christ. Come find life anew. Come in faith that all this is true. Come, now is the day of deliverance from your bondage to the devil," I was shouting over the music.

Minutes went by. No one moved. No one made a sound. Then one young woman against the back wall began sobbing and walked toward the stage. A cowboy walked forward with his hat in his hands covering his face. A kid came smiling. A brushy faced old man hobbled to the front, shouting, "Hallelujah." Some folks laughed, but even those were laughing without mocking, but with joy. The man yelled even louder, "Hallelujah." The crowd echoed his cry, "Hallelujah." The windows rattled and dust fell from the chandeliers.

I cried real big tears, tears of joy. Miss Evelyn moved to the stairs and joined the growing crowd at the foot of the stage. The Presbyterian preacher joined her in providing counsel to those seeming to be sobbing out of control and answer any questions put to them.

One laughing couple asked, "Can we be baptized now?"

The pastor said the river was a good place and began a march to the river that stopped at the first horse trough. First, at my request, the pastor slid me under the surface of the water and then I moved across the street to another trough and began baptizing all those who were willing. Cries of, "Thank you, Jesus," and "Hallelujah" were heard as the seemingly endless lines of people were dipped in the mossy waters of the troughs.

After an hour, I noticed that the lines were down and a crowd was standing around, many of them dry as a bone. I jumped to stand on a hitching rail and pulled myself up on the roof of the shade over the wooden sidewalk, where I shouted, "Come to the waters in faith all you sinners. Know the true God of this world. Live the life He designed for you." I wasn't letting anybody miss the invitation and kept beckoning as the dry individuals slowly walked away or went crying to the trough.

When it was apparent that the folks were not going home, but were standing around praying, singing, or just plain watching, I began the sermon I had prepared for this night. The street before me squirmed with live bodies trying to hear the Word. More people were caught up in the excitement and some were even directed to the trough where the Presbyterian preacher continued to baptize all that agreed to the Sacrament.

At 1 AM, a local deputy from the City Marshall's office walked up to a position beneath me as I stood on the roof, "Sir, I must ask you to stop preaching and allow these folks to go home. We do have a noise ordinance and there have been complaints. There are also laws against blocking the street and holding a parade without a permit."

"My apologies, I didn't note the time was so late."

"I'll give you fifteen minutes to disperse this crowd," the deputy added with a smile.

I spoke a few words and said a long prayer of thanksgiving before notifying all present that it was time to get out of the road and go home.

The crowd slowly dispersed with much cheering and singing as they went. Miss Evelyn was found seated on the edge of the sidewalk, sobbing. She answered my query with, "I'm just so happy."

I took her arm and led her to the caravan.

Father wasn't home. Pushing aside the canvas drapes, I crawled under the caravan and crashed into my blankets thinking I would hunt for him in the morning. I chuckled when I realized it was already early morning and shut my eyes.

I yelled and pounded on the bottom of the caravan, "He didn't come home. We need to find him." She used a boot to thump to acknowledge the call and crawled out of bed. Once dressed, I moved out from under the caravan and wondered which saloon or brothel I would find my father in this time.

Evelyn opened the side window of the caravan, "How much longer you going to keep hunting him down every other morning?"

"Until he's dead or breaks the habit. Or, he could be hit by the truth of all those sermons he preached as a phony and then we could work together."

"That would surely be miracle."

I smiled wide at that, "No more than my change and last night."

"Yeah, you're right." She paused, "Well, go find him. I'll get dressed and get us some breakfast. Oh, did you bring the bucket home?"

"No. I'll look for that, too."

I trotted down the hill to the opera house. The bucket was there by the back door, but there was only one silver dollar in it. The silver dollar went in a pocket and the bucket was left at the back door. The nearest saloon was two doors down. No one was there.

I knew then it was going to be a long search and started walking.

Seven saloons and two brothels later, I met the deputy from the night before. "What you doin' out here at this hour? The preaching don't start till dark, does it?"

"You're right. Dark. I'm looking for my father. Heavy man, white hair, clean shaved, about your height. Wear's black broadcloth suits most of the time."

The deputy stepped back. "I know where he is. I was just coming to see ya about your daddy."

"Problems?"

"Not for me anymore."

"What's that supposed to mean?"

"I think your father is at the funeral parlor."

"Is he trying to do the services or something?"

"No," he paused and took his hat off, "He's dead."

8

My throat tightened up so bad it took me awhile before I could squeeze out, "How?"

"Got in a gun fight with a bad man gambler over a floozy."

"Sounds like my father. How'd it happen?" Tears filled my eyes so bad the deputy was nothing but a blur in front of me.

The deputy looked around. "Let's go in that café. I could use a cup a coffee and maybe breakfast."

As the tears began to roll down my cheeks, I pulled out the silver dollar and said, "I've got a dollar. I'll buy." The sobs hit so bad he had to take my arm and guide me to a chair.

By the time the eggs and bacon, flapjacks, honey, and a slab of beef was set in front of the two of us to enjoy, the cups that had been filled three times, I got myself over the first shock. The deputy saw I was calmer and told me the story.

The elder Fount, my father, had been in a notorious saloon on the edge of Denver. The poker game was wild and high stakes. The barmaid had brought another round of drinks to the drunken Right Reverend Fount and he grabbed her, pulling her into his lap. The gambler across the table told him to let her go. He refused. The gambler got up and smacked the retired phony preacher with his gun, knocking him to the ground. My father challenged him to a duel for his honor. The gambler provided him with a gun and then stepped out the back door. The gun was empty, the gambler's wasn't. Three shots were fired and only one hit Preacher Fount. It was a good one, a quarter inch over his right eye, taking half his head off. He died instantly.

I felt the catch in my throat and worked hard to hold back more tears. My father would never have another chance to change his ways. "He's going to Hell, most likely. He never caught on that what he was preaching was the real thing. He's going to Hell for eternity," I sobbed and went on rambling for a while until I just stopped, ran out of steam, was drained, however you want to say it.

I looked up at the deputy who was quietly sipping his coffee, "I'd like to go make arrangements after we finish here. Which parlor has him?"

The deputy slurped another slug of the acidic coffee before saying, "It's just down the block and around the corner. I'll walk ya down there. Need a formal identification for my report on the murder. That gambler is going to swing from the county gallows, my friend."

"If I forgive him will that change anything? He killed my dad, but they were both wrong and I gotta forgive."

"No. Would you really forgive the man who killed your father?"

"Yes I would. Jesus said that we will be forgiven like we forgive. He has forgiven me of a bunch of sins. I believe I can forgive like Him and be alright with the court's ruling." I turned to the meal, carefully cut a fair sized hunk of beef and put it in my mouth. It was the first bite I tasted of that meal.

"Don't think I could do that, Preacher Daniel. Matter of fact, I'm sure I couldn't do that."

"A week ago I couldn't have done it either. Let me tell ya why I can now."

Twenty minutes later the deputy said, "Maybe someday I'll think that way, but not just now."

"Don't wait too long. Come to the meeting tonight and I'll tell ya more."

In the funeral parlor, the Right Reverend Lawrence P. Fount was laid out on a marble slab boosted four feet off the ground by two marble pedestals looking right peaceful and dead. His head was covered with a cloth. "He died instantly, young Daniel, instantly," was the mortician's opening remark.

"That's my father? I want to see his face," was all I could say for a few moments.

"Son, when a man is shot with a .44 in the back of the head, there is no face."

The deputy introduced the mortician, Ev Biscotti. "He's the best there is in this town."

"Why thank you, Tor. I'll put that in my next flier."

The mortician said, "It's a shame he had to die like that, shot in the back of the head is painless, though."

"Back of the head?" It finally sunk in enough for a comment by the deputy.

"Why yes, the bullet went all the way through. When I got to cleaning him up, it was easy to tell that it went in the back and out the front."

The deputy said, "You sure?"

"Oh, yes, quite."

"That puts a bit of a different light on the argument that Bixby has. He says they stepped off the paces and then turned and fired. The preacher here supposedly fired first, but we found the gun had no casings left in it and didn't smell like it had been fired recently. Bixby fired three times at him." The deputy stopped and thought for a moment or two, "I knew that was a lie, because this man bled out not six feet from the back door. Ole Bixby really wanted a sure thing then, an empty gun and shot in the back. Ain't never heard of anything surer when it comes to winning a gun fight. He'll hang, no doubt of that." Tor turned and walked outside where he sat on the steps writing his notes while he waited.

When I finally came out, I turned toward the caravan without even seeing the deputy.

"Was that your father, Daniel."

"Yeah, I checked the stuff Mr. Biscotti took from his pockets and the rings on his fingers," I held my hand out showing three rings, "It was him."

The deputy jotted down his affirmation. "What you gonna do now, Daniel."

"Preach the Word and try to live like Jesus."

"Man, you sure do have that stuff stuck in your head don't you?"

"Sure do. Makes life easier." I turned and kept on walking.

The deputy went to the office to file his report with the marshal, knowing he would have to go get the gambler, Bixby. As he walked he thought of how he could set up a fake breakaway by Bixby so he could simply kill the man and save the city a lot of money and trouble, but then the words Daniel had said to him stopped him cold. Something about forgiving those that hurt you the worst. Not his normal way of thinking. He'd have to think on that.

By sundown, the gambler was in jail, alive, Tor was sitting in row four on the aisle, I was ready for the night's service, the place was packed, and Miss Evelyn was warming up to sing, 'Amazing Grace,' always a favorite of every crowd. The pianist began playing as Miss Evelyn strolled onto the stage from the wings.

As the pianist reached the second time through the melody, Evelyn began singing. The crowd went quiet and listened.

I got up from my knees in the wings as she hit verse three. By verse four I was ready, standing behind the wing curtain with a Bible in hand, something I had not always done before. The song ended as Evelyn sang verse one again ending it with a repeat of, 'But now I see.'

The applause was tremendous.

I waited until it began to die before stepping out.

The room went silent.

I began with, "Tonight we will see. We will see," paused, took a deep breath, and gave them the words that God had given the world in His book about the blind seeing.

An hour later the crowd was getting antsy. I felt it. I stopped and prayed.

The piano player played slow and soft, 'Amazing Grace.' I invited them to come to the front and speak with Him or maybe even the pastor from the night before who was sitting down front center. Miss Evelyn began to sing quietly, so quietly that the back rows could not even hear her, but they knew she was singing.

The deputy was the first one to meet me at the front. I threw an arm over the man's shoulders and said, "Are you ready to be God's' man?"

"No. I'm only here to protect you. The gambler escaped and swore he would kill you before he was caught again. He also stated he would never be put in jail again. You and me need to be careful."

"I will. Why don't you move up on the stage and keep your eyes on the whole crowd and then those who want to can get down here to me."

"I'll be watching."

Nothing more happened until early the next morning when I heard Evelyn scream in the caravan above. I rolled out of bed and through the canvas curtains that gave privacy. A scuffle was going on in the caravan. I ran to the back and threw open the door to see Evelyn being pounded by the fists of an angry man.

"Where is that lying phony? I'm gonna kill him just like I killed that phony reverend of a preacher," the man yelled in the face of the cowed woman.

I said a quiet tone I really didn't feel, "I am here."

The man turned and leaped. I ducked allowing the man to fly over me and onto the ground. I spun around and leaped on top of the man. The man sliced my arm with a knife I had not seen. Grabbing the man's wrist and I twisted his entire arm in a direction the arm was never designed to bend. The man dropped the knife and kneed me in the groin. I fell back blood from the cut running down my arm and some serious pain.

In the background, Evelyn was screaming, "Kill the man."

I looked to see Evelyn bleeding from the face and standing in her tattered gown which left nothing to the imagination. "Go inside," I yelled, swinging at the attacker.

"I'll kill you just like I did your father, kid." The man spit at my face, but missed, the plug of tobacco dribbled down the front of the gambler's vest.

"I don't think so. I am not drunk or helpless. Surrender and you'll get a fair trial."

The man swung a roundhouse blow that missed as I stepped inside to deliver two heavy blows to the killer's flabby gut. The man fell back.

I followed hitting him with blow after blow, continuing even after the man was on his back in the dirt as I said, "Surrender. Surrender. Surrender."

A hand came from nowhere and spun me around, pushing me to the ground and away from the bleeding gambler.

The deputy said, "That's enough. He's out."

The deputy walked the two steps to the gambler and grabbed his arm to pull him up. The man offered no resistance. He offered nothing. The gambler was dead.

The deputy looked at me, "He's dead. You finished him and did the city of Denver a huge favor."

I could not believe my ears. "No, he can't be dead. I can't kill a man. All I did was hit him with my fists. God will not forgive me for murder," I rambled. The rambling went on even after Evelyn, wrapped in a robe, took me in her arms.

"Daniel, he was going to kill us both. You had to do it, or we both would be dead. Don't you understand, you were defending me. The Bible says believers are to defend the weak and helpless."

"It doesn't say to kill the attackers. Cain slew Abel with a rock and God condemned him."

"Sometimes you have to when they offer no other way. You tried to get him to surrender and he refused. He chose to die rather than surrender to trial and hanging. Now his only judgment will be before God."

The deputy stood up from his examination of the body, "One of your punches caught him in the nose. His nose bone was driven up into his brain. I'll bet you never thought a punch in the face would kill him."

"No. He died from my fist. I killed him. Killing is wrong."

"Would you have him kill me?" Evelyn asked.

"No."

"Do you know how many other men like your father this man has killed one way or another?"

"No."

"He has killed over twenty that we know of. All have been clouded with lies good enough that we have never been able to hang him. This town is better off without him, you can bet on that."

"I don't bet on people's lives."

"Yes you do. Every time you preach you are betting that some of the folks listening will take to your message and become Christians just like you. Some you win and some you lose."

"I win nothing. God wins it all."

"Fine. I won't argue the religious stuff with you."

I walked to the caravan door and went inside, emerging a few minutes later with rough clothes on and tucking a small sack of coins in my pocket. "I am going to the mountains to pray and think this through."

I ducked under the caravan and returned with a Bible.

"Evelyn, the caravan and all that is left in it are yours. I will find you one day in a couple weeks or more and we will discuss the future. Deputy, where can I find a good horse at a fair price?"

Evelyn grabbed his arm, "All this is good for nothing without you."

"There's enough in the safe to keep you for as long as I will be gone. If I were you, I'd find a nice boarding house for ladies and stay there. Join up with that Pastor's church and sing in the choir. I will be back."

The deputy said, "Come on, I'll get you set up." Something caught in his throat, "You know, the first time I had to kill a man, I was riding shotgun on a gold shipment. It hit me much the same as you for altogether difference reasons. I went fishing for two months to think it through. That robber got what he had coming just as this man on the ground here got what was long overdue. Would you mind if I tagged along with you for a week or so? I need a bit of a vacation myownself."

I walked to Evelyn and threw my arms around her. "Thanks. You've been a good mother to me even if you ain't my ma. I'll be back. Don't sell the caravan just yet."

I turned to the deputy, "Where's the fishin' real good around here?"

9

A couple hours later we were riding toward the mining country around Golden and the big fish along Clear Creek. I had not used a saddle much in my life, and demanded a break at midday. "I need to get off this nag and walk on my own two feet for a spell, Tor. Besides all that, I am hungry."

"If ya wanna get down we can for a spell, but if you're hungry, you're gonna have to shoot something."

"What? You didn't pack some food?"

"Not a bite. There's a great spot to rest up about half a mile from here. See what you can shoot with that Winchester under your left leg on the way there. You take the lead." He pulled his horse off the trail and let me pass.

"Dan, that rifle is yours. Came with the rig. All you are sitting on is the outfit of Bixby. Livery man said Bixby owed him about $14 and he'd take what the man owed for the rig. I figured $14 was a good price for a horse, saddle, rifle, and whatever's in them saddlebags. Ya might wanna air out that bedroll before it gets dark. Check for bed bugs and lice and such."

I jumped off the horse. "I can't take the belongings of a man I killed. It wouldn't be right, Tor. Not right at all."

"You didn't mind the deal when I found it for you. It's just that it used to belong to Bixby. Is that the drift?"

"Yeah. I can't do this."

"Okay. So if you had walked into the livery on your own and the owner offered you this rig without you knowing where it come from, you would of turned it down. Is that right?"

"Well, no," I said.

"Then what's the problem. I didn't twist the man's arm. I didn't ask. He didn't name Bixby until after the deal was done. All he told me was a man owed him and died. I grabbed it cuz it was a great deal. Danged rifle gun alone is worth the money. Take it or walk. I'll buy it off ya. Matter of fact you still owe me the $14, you ain't paid me back yet."

"So it's your horse and rig?"

I climbed back in the saddle and said, "I'll ride your horse and riggin'. Ya wanna sell it?"

"Yes I do. $300 for the lot."

"What!"

"Well, you didn't like the deal I got for you, now it's my turn to turn a profit." The deputy was grinnin' from ear to ear.

"That ain't a profit, that's robbery, highway robbery and a swindle to match. Look at this gun. The bluing is rubbed off all along this side. The butt has a crack and it's held together with wire. This horse is ugly. The saddle is so worn I can feel the horse's backbone under the blanket that you can see through. I'll give ya $20 for the lot." I grinned back.

"You think I'd sell $300 worth of rig and horse for $20? You must be counting on divine intervention or something."

"Well, I could try asking the Lord to knock you off that horse you're on and give you a Saul moment, but He don't work that way. $25."

"Sold. I don't wanna know what a Saul moment is." He kicked his horse into a trot.

Forty yards down the trail a young elk jumped from the bushes. The rifle came up. Tor yelled, "No, you danged fool. We can't eat that much." He pulled his pistol and took the head off a large cottontail rabbit not twenty feet the other side of the trail. "That will do. Lunch time, Dan, lunch time."

He walked his horse over and reached down a long way to pick up the rabbit before he took off in a trot to the great spot he was talking about. I followed thinking, 'Don't much care for rabbit. The Right Reverend, my pa, fed me that every time the count was down.'

As the rabbit roasted, Dan filled Tor's request for an explanation of a Saul moment.

"Dang, knocked him to the ground. Made him blind. Yelled at him. And, then he used him to start new churches all over the world? Ooooweeeee. That'd be some moment in my life."

"Sure was for Saul. God even changed his name to Paul and then Paul lost his head to the Romans in the end."

"God ain't too much on protecting folks from the government, is He?"

"I don't think I want to touch that comment, my friend." I dug in my pocket, "Here's the $30 I owe ya for the rig."

"About time. I was beginning to figure the interest on the loan of that fine animal and his riggin'." Tor got up and walked to his bedroll, stuck his hand in the middle, and came out with a shiny Colt .44 in a worn holster. "Here this goes with it. Bixby's short gun. It's a good gun. Tried it myownself. Them grips are real mother-of-pearl, comes from some sea critter, and the .44 is an easy gun to find ammo for in these parts." He tossed it my way.

The rig hit the dirt when I backed up and refused to catch it.

"You lettin' that gun lay in the dirt ain't good for it. Get it on. They's some wild and woolly boys up in these mountains and we may just have an Indian or two try to steal that nag of yours."

He paused for a moment and saw that I was not going to move. He yelled, "Put it on or I won't ride with you. This country is dangerous. The critters are dangerous, grizzly and lion, and the danged people are dangerous, male and female. Put. It. On."

What else could I do, I put it on.

"That was the funniest way of putting on a rig I ever did see. Thumb and forefinger of each hand was all you used and it took you forever. Some morning when the world falls apart around us, you will need to get that on in a flash and get off all the shots you can in a hurry."

"Look, Tor. I am not used to a pistol. Never handled one and never owned one. This is Bixby's, or was Bixby's. I'm still getting used to sitting on his horse, let alone strapping on his gun rig. Look at that holster, it's got a tie down. Only folks that use them are gunslicks."

"So cut it off." Tor tossed his knife to land between the toes of my boots where it stuck in the dirt.

I cut off the tie down and stuffed the leather string in the saddle bags. "Now, show me how to use it if you're gonna make me wear it."

"You'll get your first lesson tonight. Let's move. I don't wanna camp here, too public."

Five hours later I was standing, legs spread shoulder wide, arms dangling at my side, and the sixgun on my hip loaded again after tearing the thing completely apart and putting it all back together under Tor's guidance. The gun had been well cared for by the killer. "You stand like you were watching a nice looking horse walk down the main drag."

I shuffled a bit.

"That's good. Now make a fist and open your right hand a few times."

I thought it was dumb, but I did what he told me.

"Now grab the gun butt, pull, ease the hammer back – whatever you do don't let it slip – until it clicks the second time, and then pull the trigger while you're pointing the gun at that whitish rock over there. The one on the bank of the hill."

The whitish rock came apart. "Like that?"

Tor stood in his position with his mouth open. That whitish rock was a good ten yards away or more. First shot and it was a dead rock.

"Do it again. This time get off two shots. Remember, you have to pull the hammer back for each shot."

I put the gun back in the holster. "What you want me to aim at this time?"

"How's about that branch stickin' up on that dead tree?" He pointed.

I brought the gun out with no apparent speed, two shots sounded like two shots from two guns one on top of the other like one was just a mite slower than the other. Two branches on a dead tree lying 15 yards or so away disintegrated in puffs of saw dust and bark.

"Reload," was all Tor could say.

I ejected three cases and inserted three fresh rounds from my belt. "How come?"

"Always reload as soon as you can after firing. You will never know when you might need all five shots."

"Why only five rounds? There's six holes here. In a battle wouldn't six be better?"

"How many times have your fired a pistol of any kind?"

"Just the three shots today."

"Then how can you shoot so well. You hit the target and are moderately fast in gettin' yourself in the fight. You amaze me."

"Ain't that what a man's supposed to do?" I flipped the loading gate shut and spun the cylinder. "Six shots loaded."

Tor walked over to me and stuck his hand out, "Let me have your .44."

Lifting it out of the holster, I handed it to him. "Here ya are. What's the problem?"

"Watch."

Tor walked over to the stream bed and grabbed a fist sized rock that was fairly flat on one side. He held the pistol with his hand wrapped around the grip. The hammer was down and his finger was not on the trigger. He smacked the rock into the hammer with the barrel pointed across the stream. The gun went off sending a slug to ricochet off the water and into the hillside.

"That's why."

"Well, how many times am I gonna be hitting my gun with a rock?"

"Probably never, but if you drop something on the hammer when it's in your holster, you will have a nice groove down your leg for the rest of your life, which might not be very long. A shot like that in just the right spot and you'll bleed out in a minute, or get gangrene, or lose the use of that leg due to a shattered knee, or just plain have an ugly scar on a weak leg." He handed the pistol back to me. I slipped it back in its home on my hip. "All them options are not too healthy. A working man cannot afford to carry a round under the hammer. Once you get in the battle, the first time you reload you fill them all. If you know the battle is coming, you load them all ahead of time. Got it?"

"Yes, sir. None of them options sound good to me. Don't want the battle either." I drew and shot a large rattlesnake coming out from a hole under the rock right next to Tor. "There's supper."

Tor jumped and landed about six feet away from where he started. "You eat snake?"

"Nope. Hear it's good though."

"I don't eat snake," he said as he continued to watch the reptile writhe in the dust making mud with its blood. "I'll be back in a few minutes. Get us a fire going."

"For supper?"

"Yup. You the eatin'est feller I ever rode with."

"How do you think I keep my manly figure."

Tor went hunting.

I went fishing as soon as the fire was burning well.

The fish were not biting and Tor was not back after an hour. No shot sounded and I was beginning to wonder what was happening in the woods when the shot finally came. It sounded surprisingly close.

I rounded up more wood and set the coffee to boiling as I waited. The fishing line got checked a time or two. Still no Tor. What was there to do except strap on the Bixby gun and saddle my horse. Just as I swung into the saddle, "Hey, you wanna come over here with that horse and help be bring this in."

It was Tor.

I rode the horse across the stream and up to where Tor was coming out of the woods dragging a young doe, all nicely gutted and beheaded, toward camp. I pulled it up on the horse's withers and gave Tor a hand climbing on behind him, turned the horse for camp and crossed the stream. As we were crossing, the rock I had tied the fishing line to came off the large rock it had set on.

I had a bite.

10

An hour later we were eating venison steaks in the dark and rigging a rack to make jerky on. The coffee pot was empty next to the embers of the fire when we rolled into the bedrolls for a night's sleep. Both of us were full to the brim and content.

The fish got away.

Two days later, we rode into Golden. Tor wanted to stop and see an old saddle partner and I was just going to find someplace with a couple of books for sale. Didn't make a difference what they were, I just wanted to unwind a bit in something other than the Bible. It had taken me a full day of thinking and praying to make that decision.

Tor pointed in the direction of the hotel, "Meetcha there in a couple of hours. Two beds please. You roll and toss so bad I'll end up on the floor. There's a gunsmith down the block a bit that might be able to do something about the slickness of them grips on your Colt. Try him." He rode away before I could say anything.

I was dazzled having never seen big cities this far west before, but never had I seen a town with the hustle and bustle of this one. I had to guide the horse around wagons and people walking in the middle of the street. A wagon loaded with beer from the Coors brewery almost killed a man after the wagon driver took his eyes off the street to look at a dance hall gal on the balcony of a saloon. The man turned and saw the lead horses when they were about two feet from straddling him and moved right quick to the side, almost kissing the off lead in the process.

I kept easing up the street looking for the sign advertising a hotel in the midst of all the other signs. Seems like every building had three or more businesses or products to sell that they thought each was worthy of having its own sign. "I ain't seen this many signs since St. Louis, but St. Louis never had this many folks running around like chickens with their heads cut off."

"Hey, quit star gazing and get outta the road, young feller," came from my right. A pedestrian was held up by my slow rubber necking to see all there was to see.

"Sorry, old timer, I'll get pushing this crowd a little and help us both move. How far's it to the hotel?"

"Two buildings down. Only sign is on the winder, but ya cain't miss'er a bit. Bright green paint around them winders."

"Thank ya kindly, sir."

"Now get outta my way."

The horse moved with a gentle gig of the spurs I'd found in the saddle bag. Tor said they were cavalry spurs, short and stubby, and also reckoned that Bixby had been cavalry once upon a time "Cuz he rode so straight up and down like he had a ram rod for a back bone." That horse and me pushed through the crowd until sure enough there was the green trim on a pair of fair sized windows. One said HOTEL and the other said SALOON in large gold and black letters.

We, the horse and me, had to sidle in between the hitching rail and the plank sidewalk in order to tie off the gelding I had named, Solomon. Not that the horse was wise, just that it sounded like a good Christian horse name. The horse would never have a thousand wives, but being a gelding it wouldn't matter.

I swung down gingerly due to a backside that still wasn't used to all the riding, pulling the Winchester out of its case. After doing a couple of deep squats, I entered the hotel and walked to the desk. "Need a room with two beds or two rooms with one bed."

"Very good, sir. Let me see what we have." The desk clerk turned to look at a bunch of cubbies behind him. "Aah yes, sir. We have two rooms side by side, each with one bed, both on the third floor facing the avenue. Will that do, sir."

"Yeah. How much?"

"Fifty cents each. Dinner will be served in the dining room," he pointed to a door behind me, "In about an hour. Of course, they always have something to eat 24 hours each day. There is also the Saloon to your right," again he pointed, "Serving the finest of liquors, beers, wines, and just plain everyday good whiskey. One of our local miners has a still and a local brewery makes the finest beer in the territory."

I plunked a ten dollar gold piece on the counter and said, "May I start an account and sign for meals and drinks?"

"Yes Sir, you certainly may. Sign the ledger please and use the same signature on your tabs." He turned and pulled two keys from adjoining slots, flipped a tab to red like most of the other rooms, and set the keys on the ledger as I signed, 'Daniel Fount, Denver.'

"Could you tell me where the best livery and gunsmith might be?"

"Why yes, Sir. The livery is down the alley on the right side of the hotel," he pointed, "And the gunsmith is across the street and uphill about a quarter mile. Can't miss him, he has a large six shooter for a sign hanging way out from and above the rest of the signs on this street. Old German fella that I have only met once, but the best of reputations I assure you." The clerk was a fount of information as I learned things of this town.

"Thank you."

"I recognize your gun, but you weren't the man that was wearing it last time I saw it."

"He lost in the game of life."

"Oh, very good, Sir. He was not a very savory individual. Thank you for winning in the game of life." The clerk smiled and turned to the lady that just walked in and stepped up to the counter like she owned the place. I didn't mind, the room keys were in my hand.

I heard, "Who is that terrible man? He killed a man in the saloon the last time I was here," from the lady.

As I walked to the gunsmith, I got to thinking that maybe, just maybe, it would be wise to change the grips altogether rather than just have them reworked. Tor was coming down the street, saw me, and pulled over to the plank sidewalk where he said, "You wanna double up?"

"Sure."

We finished at the gunsmith with me carrying a loaner and Tor guiding the horse to the hotel where we picked up Solomon and rode to the livery up the alley.

"Ya seen one livery stable, ya seen them all," Tor said.

"And smelled them all," I just had to add.

Two days later we left town before the sun came up and the crowds hit the streets. Tor's old saddle partner was no longer in Golden. It was Sunday. The bells were ringing on at least three churches somewhere in the town. I felt a pull, but was not ready for the questions that would come inside the walls of a friendly church. Tor offered to go with me if that was the hold up. I turned Solomon to the street all the wagons had been using coming into town.

Within an hour the sun was up, we were off the road and on a thin trail leading into the high country, and up ahead was a smoldering fire. Without saying a word, we spread out as we approached the smoke. No one was there.

A breeze picked up as Tor looked around. Nothing. A jumble of prints in the dirt told me nothing. At least four different horses had been over this site time and time again. Tor got down and started probing the ground with a stick he grabbed. I watched with the newly adorned six shooter held in position with my elbow locked into my side. No one had to tell me something had happened here and it was probably bad for somebody.

Tor finally tossed the stick, "No new graves."

"How do you know?"

"The top inch or so is disturbed by the prints here, but after that inch or so the ground is rock hard. If there was a grave the dirt would be loose and the stick would have gone in deep from the pressure I put on it. Why don't you dump your canteen on this fire so's it don't get away, fill up from the stream, and we'll just mosey on our way. While you're doin' that, I'll just take me a ride up towards them trees and see what I can see."

I did as he asked while he looked around in the direction the horses had gone. All there was in that direction was a heavily forested area leading to the base of the biggest mountain around. The whole scene seemed strange as the water gurgled out of the canteen while I watched Tor moving at a quick trot. When the gurgling quit, I rode down to the water and was just about off the horse when I saw him.

The man was sitting with his legs in the water next to a rock on the far side of the creek, still as the stone itself. A gun lay in his lap and the front of his shirt was bright red.

"Tor."

No response.

"TOR!"

I looked back to see Tor jerk his horse around and ride like the devil was after him toward the camp site. Out of the trees came three riders and as soon as I saw them they opened fire. Starting to mount, I realized that I was in a good position to cover Tor and the old man next to the rock. The rock looked like a good place to hunker down.

I crossed the creek and turned Solomon loose to fend for himself, squatted behind the rock, and then pulled the wounded man to the same cover I was in. Laying the Winchester across the top of the rock I lined up the sights and squeezed the trigger. The center of the three riders took a tumble. Tor kept coming straight across the campsite and on through the water until he jumped off his horse, rifle in hand, and took up a spot thirty feet or so downstream.

"You okay?"

"Yeah, not a scratch."

"I wanted you to come back anyhow, but not this way. Did ya have to bring your friends?"

"They got a bit pushy. Who's that you got there with you?"

"Wounded man. Still breathing, but that's about it."

Tor leaned into his rifle butt and squeezed off a round that took a horse out from under one of the riders. My following shot sent the rider tumbling. The last rider pulled up behind a large fir tree filled with moss. I couldn't see him, so I put five rounds through the tree about man high.

Tor did the same thing while I reloaded.

While I was reloading, I could hear the wounded man trying to say something. I leaned down to listen. He whispered desperately, "They took her."

"Who?"

"They took her, my daughter, they took her."

"Where?"

"North . . . uuhhh . . . west."

"What's her name?"

He tried to sit up. I held him down. "Calm down, we'll help ya."

"They took her."

"What's her name and why?"

Seeing that the man was getting weaker and weaker with every breath, I asked"What's her name?"

"Diane. Just like her . . . mother . . . Diane."

"Where would they take her?"

"The ranch. Get her back. They'll .... kill ..." He tried to sit up.

I eased him back down, "Who are they?"

He breathed a shallow breath. Blood oozed from the hole in his chest. I saw him gather himself for one more answer. "Lazy E brand. My . . .Rafter B. . . save it for her." He paused with a gasp that I thought was his death rattle. "Kill . . . Burrrrr…"

This time he did die. It was over for him.

Tor stopped firing as a horse ran out from behind the tree we had fired at. "Let's go see what's what over there." He looked at the dead man. "He still alive?"

"No. Just died. We got a problem."

11

"I don't have a problem, yet. All we gotta do is make sure those three over there are dead or gone and then do some buryin'."

"Tor, this man says they took his daughter and he has a ranch they are trying to take from her."

Nothing had moved for a while. Tor stood up so he could see the ground just over the creek bank. Nothing. "Let's ride."

'It is over,' I thought, 'I killed at least one more man. God forgive me.' I started shaking.

Tor walked his horse through the stream and up the bank into the campsite before looking back, "You comin' or you gonna stand there and feel sorry for yourself. We defended ourselves from them killers and now we gotta take care the leavin's."

I walked through the stream and started toward the fir tree I had filled full of holes. I was half way there when I remembered Solomon. The horse was off a couple hundred yards to the east grazing on the sparse grass alongside the creek. "Solomon, you'd do me a favor if you came here." I whistled.

The horse lifted his head, looking straight at me. He bowed his head for another bite and I thought I was in for a long walk to get the horse. Instead, Solomon picked up his head and started trotting toward me with his head off to one side to keep from stepping on the reins. I waited and when the horse got close I grabbed the saddle horn and climbed aboard wondering what else this horse could do.

At the fir tree, Tor was examining a bloody man on the ground. "Bout time you got here. Check them other two. This one's still alive. If them two are dead, check the horses for brands and clean out the saddlebags for letters and stuff that might tell us about these men. Did that other horse run far?"

I looked around. "Nah, he's over at the tree line munching on the grass."

"Check him out. We could use a pack horse or two."

I checked the first man. Dead. The second was still alive, but just barely. He had a round through his middle just above his belt line and another in a lung which was bubbling blood.

Hunkering down next to the man, "Fella, you are dying. Are you right with your Creator?"

"You . . some kinda . . . ijit . . or what?"

"I'm a preacher."

"You . . shot me."

"You tried to kill me. What did you expect? Would it make a difference if I said I was sorry."

The man spit in my face. "Damn you." He fell back and breathed one last breath as one last bubble popped on his chest.

"I think you are the one that is damned. I just need God's guidance in a better way to deal with men like you."

Tor eased up behind him. "My man's dead." He heard what I said and added, "What other way is there to handle men that are coming at you shooting and trying to kill you and send you to heaven?"

"I don't rightly know. Me and God will have a couple of long discussions about this."

"Daniel, why do you think God gave you the gift of being able to hit a fly in the eye at fifty paces with a sixgun and take out a running rabbit with a Winchester at a hundred?"

"So I can eat."

"You really mean that don't you. You're not just talkin'?"

"Yeah."

"Did you ever think that maybe God wants a Christian man to stand up for the weak and take care of the feeble, the orphans, the women, and such?"

"Well, yeah. Been thinking and praying on that, but God has done no answerin' yet."

Tor swept his arm around the whole scene before them and said, "You really believe this isn't God speaking. What's it gonna take? You waiting for Him to boom out of the clouds with words loud and clear?"

"That would be nice and definite, wouldn't it?"

"Yeah, but I don't think He works that way. He's a bit more subtle. He sends three killers after you while you're helping an old man die. He tells you there's a weak woman off someplace in trouble, a woman that can lose her ranch. We don't even know if there're kids involved. Matter of fact, we don't know that the woman is a woman and not a snotty nosed kid still."

"Let's bury these four bodies and get on up the trail of the rest of the killers."

"Sounds like a good idea. We done took care of a bunch of killers and put a dent in the forces of evil what took the gal. Come to think on that, did you think you were fighting evil here just as much as you would be in the tent or the opry hall or wherever? Too bad we don't have Miss Evelyn here to make for a nice send off for these three hoodlums and specially the old man over there."

"Shut up." I grinned. "Let's get the burying done. You dig and I'll say the words over their graves."

"You help dig and I'll listen to the words. How's that?"

"What we gonna dig with? This dirt's hard as a rock and filled with rocks."

"Let me look around." He rode off toward the trees.

I caught up the only horse standing and finished one that was wounded too bad to save. There was a bit of jerky and some piñon nuts in one set of bags and nothing else but a few rounds of ammo and a clean shirt. Tor claimed the shirt and split up the ammo.

The sun was low on the horizon as the last two rocks were set on the grave. "I really wish we could have given the old man his own grave and not had to bury him with his killers."

"Forget it. There was just this one big knocked down tree I could find. They all fit in the root hole and there was a mess of rocks up close. They are dead. You told me yourself as we laid them to rest, these are just casing for their souls and the souls are gone. God will pick them up later."

"I guess you could say it thataway, but I still don't like it."

"Daniel, when you get to likin' killin' and buryin', it's time for you to hang up your gun and spend the rest of your days praying." Tor pointed toward the horses. "Let's mount up and git. By the way, I like what that gunsmith did with the grips on your gun. That engraved cross in blood red says a lot about the man carrying the gun."

"It gives me a good grip, but I think it's a bit dramatic."

"Not for the showman of the Lord that you are."

"I ain't nothin' but a servant in the Lord's house."

"Well now, let me do some figurin' here. The Lord's house is the Church, right?"

"Well, yeah, you could call it that."

"And the servants of the Church are called Deacons, right?"

"Yeah. They were set up to help the weak widows and orphans."

"So that makes you a Deacon, don't it?"

"I guess you could say that. All I want is to be a servant of the Lord."

"Okay, Deacon, you got yourself a name."

"What? You're gonna change my name?"

"Yup. God did that with Abram and Saul when they started working for Him. Why not you? I like the ring to the name, Deacon."

"I ain't too sure, Tor. I ain't really cut out to be helpin' widows and orphans and such."

"Which piece is missing?"

The Deacon didn't have an answer.

After tying two saddles to the saddle on the one standing horse, and making sure the guns were tied on tight, we rode into the trees with rifle butts on our thighs, leading our new packhorse. The tracks led us not more than a hundred yards into the trees before turning left and following the terrain through the trees until they cut to the right and uphill along a cut with a small trickle of water flowing, and up over a pass a ways past the spring that fed the trickle.

Once over the pass, Tor called a halt for the night. "Gonna be too dark to see the track right soon and I'm getting' a mite hungry."

"I'm beyond hungry."

12

Sunrise was blocked by the mountain, making for a cool morning. The trail of the killers went off before us like a beacon on a rocky shore, but neither of us was in a hurry. The Lazy E brand on the pack horse matched the brands on the two dead horses, so the assumption was that the Lazy E was the outfit that had killed the old man and run off with Diane. Tor had never heard of either brand and figured they had to be from a distance away.

"Let's go easy and slow, Deacon. Any place we can't see too far ahead is a good place for an ambush. By now they know that their three shooters didn't finish their task. My guess is they were supposed to finish off the old man and make him disappear. The hands they were riding with will be wondering how a wounded and dying old man could take the three of them. I'm guessing they will just keep on riding, or send one really good man back to see what's what."

"Tor, could we quit with the Deacon stuff.? I'm just simply a Daniel."

"There ain't nothin' simple about you, Deacon, nothin' at all. Daniel's lions didn't open their mouths and weren't dangerous. You are dangerous. You don't know it yet, but you could probably win in a gunfight with better than half the gundummies running around this countryside. You are dangerous. I'm glad I'm on your side and you're on God's side. Let's ride. I wanna get down off the steep part of this mountain. We got nowhere to go 'cept down the trail and that's like being in a funnel."

"Wanna help me get this horse packed up?"

At the bottom of the steep grade the trail split three ways; right, left, or straight ahead. The tracks went straight ahead and Tor indicated he was happy with that. There was flat land out there no more than a mile away. A line of dust was very pronounced at the base of the mountains on the other side of the flats.

Tor said as we began forward, "We're in for a long ride. Them folks ain't lettin' no moss grow on their horses hooves. There's a five building, two horse town up this valley a couple hours away. Let's head up there, sell the extra horse and gear, and see what we can get to eat. We might also pick up a bit of gossip or news concerning the Rafter B or the Lazy E. Sooner or later we are going to end up at one or the other. Maybe even both."

I started down the trail while Tor continued to survey the countryside in all directions, even up behind where we had come from.

The sign said, 'BLACK – no Chinee allowed' which kinda gave the idea these folks might not be the friendliest folks we had ever met. It was an assumption that panned out when the man at the stable said, "I don't want the horse. Wouldn't have a Lazy E horse if I was lost and afoot. You boys out to get hung or something?"

Tor gave him an earful before saying, "Where is that ranch, anyhow?"

"Way up over yonder. Northeast of that tall peak over there. I only see'd them once down this far and that were three days ago. One of them riders, there was nine of them, wanted to drink up all the booze in town and the others wanted to help. Some fella traveling down valley, gave one of them boys some lip. They just up and hung him. Right there crossed the street. Tossed a rope up over the center beam of that there cabin and jerked him up. Big fella he was, took four of them pullin' on the rope to get him off the ground half a foot. Big guy danged near kicked that front wall in. You can see the marks from his boots and the blood from his bleeding fingers where he tried to get a holt of that wall. Died anyway. Them there riders just laughed at the whole danged thing. Missy tried to stop them. They slapped her around a bit and then two of them took her out behind the cabin and Missy won't say nothin' past that. She's forty years old and been a widow for the past five. She just sits in her cabin now and cries a lot."

"How far away is that Lazy E?"

"I ain't got the foggiest idee."

I said, "Would Miss Missy talk with a preacher?"

"You bet she would."

I turned and went to the cabin.

Tor walked over to the largest building in town carrying the extra guns and gear. The sign said, 'General Mechandise.' He came out with a tater sack full of cans and whatever. He still carried one hand gun the proprietor did not want. Someone's initials were carved in the notched grips. It was a .44 identical to my gun except for the grips. Tor bummed a screwdriver from the livery man and took the grips off, tossing them in the potbellied stove in the corner of the livery office. He tucked the skeleton gun in his bed roll. There was a sly grin on the man's face.

After I left Miss Missy's house, she was standing in the door with a smile on her face. "Daniel, you take care of yourself and find them gun hands. They need someone to read to them from the Good Book and you are just the man."

"Thank you, Missy. I just do the work of the Lord."

"That won't be pleasant work, Deacon," yelled Tor.

"Let's get on up that other hill." I was anxious to get on with it.

The next morning the rains came.

"This will wipe out the tracks we need."

"Don't worry about it. I prayed last night that God would deliver these gunmen to our hands without a fight. I got the impression He said yes."

"Oh, goodie, now we're working on impressions." Tor threw up his arms, "Okay, I'm game. Let's go round them up."

"He didn't say we would just round them up. He said He would deliver them into our hands."

We crested another pass where we found two men stone drunk snoring away. Three empty bottles lay in the coals of last night's fire. I walked up to the two men and relieved them of their guns before kicking them awake while Tor stood at the edge of the camp with his rifle covering the scene.

The two came up on their feet trying to draw sixguns that were not present in the location they had been every other morning of their lives. "Looking for these?" I asked, holding one in each hand pointing at each belly.

"Wha? Where? I, aaahh. Everson's gonna kill you if you mess with us."

"Who is Everson?" Tor asked with a soft voice.

"My boss. Runs the Lazy E, biggest ranch in the State of Colorado and Wyoming."

"There's some fair sized ranches south of here and I know of at least one that's bigger than Texas over on the Kansas/Nebraska border. That must be some big ranch you come from." Tor's face got hard, "How come I never heard of a mess of rattlesnakes that big? You two the really bad men that messed with Miss Missy back there in Black."

"That old bag, she . . ."

Tor stopped the comment by stepping forward and giving the man the butt of one of the sixguns in a powerful upper cut. The man went down like a shooting star only without the brilliance.

I knelt down alongside the poleaxed man. "He's dead. From the angle of his head, I'd say ya busted his neck, Tor."

The second man layed back down and started shaking and holding his head. "Oh, my head. It's gonna blow up. I think we got some bad Rye back there. My head. It's killin' me."

I said, "Save us the trouble," and kicked the man in the back, "Get up and get your horses saddled."

"I can't."

In a split second, my gun was in his mouth. The hammer was drawn back and I had my finger on the trigger. "Last chance. Saddle up your horse, we got a trail to ride and you're gonna show it to us."

"Not me. Kill me if you want, but I ain't gonna show you nothin'."

Tor jammed a sixgun barrel in the man's ear. "Wanna bet which one of us can take the biggest chunk outta his head, Deacon?"

"Well, let me see, Tor. Both of us are packin' .44's here. One's got a short barrel and the other is long. So if we both pull the trigger at the same time, my bullet will get there first. If I angle the barrel up slightly, there won't be nothin' for you to blast off."

"That's a great theory. You wanna try it?"

"How we gonna tell which got the biggest chunk."

"The splatter."

"The splatter?"

"Yeah. If I get the biggest chunk of the splatter of his brains and skull will be to your right. Whereas, you get the bigger chuck, the splatter will be to your front. Got it?"

"Yeah. On three. One. Two."

"Wait. I'll take ya there. You will die and I will blow both your brains out, if you have brains that is."

"Saddle up and tie your partner on his horse well. I'm assuming we've a ways to go."

"Couple of days or more just to the southern boundary of the Lazy E. A week to the headquarters." The man said as he got up to saddle up.

Me. I had some reservations on the truthfulness of the man's times, but said nothing.

The man moaned and bellyached for the next six hours as we traveled northeast. "Come on. Let's get some sleep so I can sleep off this hangover. That was some bad Rye, I ain't never had a head like this one."

"What? I thought you were born with that head," Tor chided the man. "It's so ugly and danged near worn out. But, that's all right, you won't be needing it much longer."

The man just gave him an evil eyed look.

We camped a half mile past a small stream that was too much in the open for Tor's happiness.

The man started, "That Missy gal, she was . . ."

Tor finished it with a sharp right to the jaw that put the man to sleep.

He woke up hours later tied to the blanket wrapped body of his partner and screamed.

"Shut up or I'll lay you out permanently," was Tor's reply.

Silence followed.

13

We dropped off the dead man with a sheriff in a small town. The sheriff pointed out that the man had a bounty on his head, a fair sized one. The sheriff promised to wire the sheriff that offered the bounty and would have an answer for us on the way back. I preached at the man's funeral after his partner dug the grave and Tor laid him in it.

The Sheriff said at the end, "I hope you boys have some warm blankets. The pass and twenty miles beyond will freeze ya in the height of summer and no one in their right mind goes up there in the winter. I got a couple of blankets a saddle bum left behind when he chose to die in our little town."

"How'd he died."

"Chicken pox, the doc said. I think every man, woman, and child had the chicken pox after he passed. You want the blankets or no?"

"I'll pass. I heard the Indians got all kinds of diseases from the blankets the army gave them. I don't want no chicken pox." Tor could be real definite when he needed to be.

"Well, you boys keep a look out for them Lazy E cowboys. They think they own the range. Truth is the Rafter B has more lawful range than the Lazy E. Rafter B owns most of the water rights also."

"That could just be that's what all this is about," I said. "Did they pass through here in the last week or so with a female?"

"They ain't welcome in our town and they know it. Last time they was here and had a hurrah in our town they killed the youngest son of one of our families. Six years old and shot cuz he wouldn't pick up the gun a randy threw down for him. Seems the boy bumped into this randy and the randy was insulted. Demanded that the boy draw. Folks pointed out the kid didn't have no gun, so the randy threw one down. Finally, the randy got egged on long enough; he just drew and killed the kid. We hung three of them. Two of the ones we hung had prices on their heads in Cheyenne. Them Lazy E hands ain't been back since."

The grave digging partner said, "They comin' back. You just wait and see. No one hangs the Lazy E."

"It's been six months and they ain't tried. I'd be happy to hang this one if you wanna leave him." The sheriff looked at Tor. "I can get him outta your hair that way."

Tor was thinking heavy on it when I said, "Nah. We need him to find the headquarters of this Lazy E ranch."

"Well," said the sheriff, "Ya can't miss it. It's the poorest lookin' property you ever did see up thataway about thirty miles. It's so cold on that side of the pass, ain't no cows will stick around. They all head south in a hurry. Don't you worry none, the stench will announce it for you."

"Sounds like a glorious ranch." I was trying hard to see a place like this in my mind. This country was so beautiful I was having a hard time.

Tor cut in, "Let's ride. We can get a good ten miles before we have to camp which should put us at the ranch by noon tomorrow."

The sun started the new day with a sky painted by God in one of His better efforts. I washed the sleep from my eyes with a bandana after dipping it in a stream.

The grave digger was getting antsy on us. "You gotta let me go. If I ride in there with you, they'll hang me after they kill you."

"Sounds like real friendly folks on that ranch you work for. How many cows they running?"

"Don't rightly know. Must be around ten or twelve thousand. We brought in one lot from Wyoming last year that musta had three thousand head in it. Man was that a ride. We almost killed the cows moving them south that fast."

"What'd you do? Steal them in Wyoming?"

"Nah. We got them in Montana. Lost a good one in ten on the way down."

Tor looked at me. "This must be one mighty big rustling outfit. Must run them to Nebraska to sell."

"Nah. We moves'em to Kansas. Nobody knows Montana brands in Kansas."

"We're in deeper than we thought, Tor. How we gonna deal with this?"

"God said He'd deliver, right?"

"Yup."

"Then we will wait upon this God of yours."

I looked at the grave digger and said, "There's smoke up ahead. That the ranch."

"Naw, that's a line shack, and I do mean shack. I spent a week snowed in there last year. Nearly froze to death. You could throw a cat through the cracks in them walls. Ain't been chinked since forever."

"How many men there now?"

"Maybe two, at worst three. Only two bunks."

Tor said, "Is there a way around it?"

"Yeah, but it's a long way and you don't wanna go there."

"How long?

"Two days."

I said, "Let me just ride down there and ask for a job."

"Sounds like a plan," Tor said.

"They'll kill ya." The grave digger was right cheery to have around.

"I'll give it a try. I ain't never been killed before."

We decided we'd all go and then rode on down to have a friendly visit.

As they approached, a man stepped out of the cabin with a tin cup in his hand. "Howdy fellas." He looked at the grave digger, "Welcome back, Ethan. We been a missin' ya."

"These men killed Frank. Kill'em."

"Frank probably deserved to die, foolin' with women the way he does. Never could stand a man that fooled with women that didn't wanna be fooled with. Like you, Ethan. You kill your own snakes, I ain't gonna help ya." He looked to Tor and said, "What's up with you two hangin' out with this scum?"

Ethan looked at Tor with fear in his eyes. He knew how Tor felt about him and now he was getting no support from the brand. "I guess I'll just let them kill ya then Peso. Ya oughta be dead anyhow. Never did like ya none," whined Ethan.

"How many men this ranch got? I need a job and I need a warm place for the winter."

"Boss man ain't around, but I can tell ya he ain't hiring the likes of you."

"Why not. I'm a better hand than anyone he's ever seen. If you can saddle it, I can ride it."

"Cuz you the law. I seen ya in Denver last spring when I went in to spend my winter money." He reached for his gun.

My shot slammed him back through the open doorway and into the cabin just as the window glass broke and a rifle barrel appeared. Tor and I sent lead through the window taking out the glass that was left. The sound of a body hitting dirt and a man's cry of pain put a period on the episode.

"I'll check inside. You keep an eye on this clown," Tor said as he headed for the door, leaving his horse ground reined. He grabbed Peso's foot and drug him out of the way before sticking his sixgun in the door, "Speak up or I'll poke holes in ya if ya move."

He stepped in.

"All down."

I stepped down from Solomon and started for the cabin. Ethan took the opportunity, slapped his horse's rump with the reins, and took off for places unknown. I let him ride until he was out a long rifle shot away before sending a couple of pistol shots in his direction. Ethan fell from the horse.

"Danged if that ain't the best pistol shot I ever did see," exclaimed Tor.

"I was just trying to scare him so's he'd keep goin'. Never figured on hitting him."

"I'll bet he's scared where he ends up. That ole devil ain't gonna take kindly to the likes of him polluting Hell."

"There's a lot of his old friends to keep him company in the misery and pain of an eternal fire that burns but does not consume."

"Let's ride. Folks might a heard them shots."

Rather than go directly toward the smoke we had been seeing for miles, we rode to the east where a small group of mountains stuck up their heads. "Time to check out the rest of the place from a distance before we go in."

Tor was all in favor of that and led the way.

Wasn't long until a group of six riders could be seen heading for the cabin where the three bodies were sprawled in their own blood. A saddled horse trotted out to greet them. Tor led us into a wash that was deep enough to keep us hidden from the new arrivals for at least a mile if we had wanted to go downhill toward the headquarters, but we went up hill toward the mountains and ran out of cover in a few hundred yards.

I said, "Let's just wait right here and see what they do."

Tor agreed. "You know something. You got that gun of yours out right quickly back there. Mine was not even moving upward when your shot went by my ear. Ya plugged him dead center, too."

"Didn't think or I would have let you kill him. I still ain't too sure how God's gonna take this killin' stuff."

"I'm happy you got him. His gun was almost clear of the holster when your slug nailed him. God knows you saved my miserable life."

"Let's don't dwell on my shooting. I just reacted. I didn't plan to kill nobody. He moved. He died. That's about all there was to it. God delivered them." To himself he thought, 'God deliver me for the killin'.'

Tor shook his head as he watched the six riders toss three bodies over three horses and head back to the ranch. "Come dark, I propose we sidle on down there and follow the tracks to take a look see. That'll mean some walkin'. You up to some walkin'?"

"In the dark is evil. Men hide their sins in the dark. We as God's people are the light of the world and it's time to shine a bit of light on that mess of rattlesnakes."

Knowing that six alive and three dead hands were headed for the ranch, the two of us set out to find a very quiet corner in the mountains where we could keep an eye on things and get rested for the night work. When we found it, Tor set me to watching for a couple of hours while he napped with the understanding we'd trade tasks in two hours. Or, we'd do what was necessary if it all fell apart. "Plans ain't worth spit unless the other side cooperates, Deacon. You remember that."

"Yes sir. Hush up and get some shuteye."

14

I awoke to a dark sky and a quiet campsite. Tor was nowhere in sight and I, sure as all get out, wasn't about to start yelling for him. A quick check found Tor's horse was still tied to the line we had set up for the three horses. His saddle was on the ground and his bed was still laid out like he had just gotten up from it.

I stepped into the brush to relieve myself. When I returned to camp Tor was there whittling on a long, straight limb. "Where ya been?" asked Tor.

"In the bushes, uh, lookin' for you."

"I was over on this other side doin' the same thing. Them boys down there like big fires, look at that baby."

I had to move a bit to see the yard of the ranch headquarters. It was lit up like midday. Men were moving around with a purpose. "I wonder why."

"Simple. They think we might be coming in to join them for one reason or another."

I kept looking mesmerized by the fire that far away.

"Don't stare at it. You'll have a blind spot in your vision for a while if you do." Tor was not a happy deputy from the tone. "I do know that they have something in that small shack to the right of the biggest shack that they want to keep. There's a man stationed on each side of it. Every once in a while someone comes over and looks in the window. Big guy down there, big around that is, must be the boss. He seems to be grabbing men from time to time and sending them on their way to do something or be somewhere."

"Any way we can get to the big shack? We torch it and we just might be able to get to the smaller shack in the ballyhoo." I was not happy with the situation. It looked like more killing to me, a lot more killing.

"Ballyhoo. Where'd you ever get a word like that?"

"Miss Evelyn. She had quite an education before the death of her family put her on another line of work."

"She's a pretty lady. Sings nice, too."

"She is a lady. Wasn't always, but is now."

"Who cares about what folks were yesterday? I surely don't. I just hope I'm alive tomorrow so I can continue to learn new and greater things." Tor was looking into the night sky as he spoke. "You still gotta teach me about this God of yours who can be a Father, the Son, and a Ghost all at the same time and in the same place."

"Wow. You, a philosopher. Let's make war on these men. And remember, God will deliver them."

Both of us looked at the thirty or so men running around like ants whose hole had been flooded. Neither of us was too happy with what he saw. "Deacon. I reckon that gal is in that cabin."

"You wouldn't kid me, now would you? I agree. Let's go get her."

"Yeah. If we leave now, we got time to do what we need to do in the dark. We'll lead our horses and leave them as close to the shacks as we safely can and continue walking the rest of the way."

Moments passed as we rolled up beds and loaded horses with saddles and the rest of the camp things. The third horse was free of any kind of a load. "Deacon, I can ride as well bareback as I can in a saddle. So, when we get the gal she gets my horse with the saddle."

"I hope she ain't wearing a dress."

They walked.

The fire was still blazing as we watched men throw logs on it. Every once in a while a major plume of sparks would fly and produce a series of eerie shadows all around the fire. Men would laugh or make ghost sounds, or at least what they thought were ghost sounds, into the dark.

Tor signaled a halt, "This is as close as I want to travel draggin' a horse. Let's take a good look and set up the details to this plan."

I was trembling inside a bit. "I ain't too sure this is a good idea. How we gonna do anything without killing a mess of men?"

"Let's work on that."

We spent 20 minutes watching what was going on until I said, "There's only about 18 men down there now."

"The boss musta put a dozen to bed cuz he figures he's gonna need some sharp men in the morning. I figure we got till an hour before sunup to act. They'll be set for the good old Indian trick of a dawn attack. What's your plan, Preacher."

"Just a deacon, a servant of the Church." I was testy. "My idea would be for one of us to go around the camp down there, come up on that shack where the gal is from the back, the dark side, and the other stays here to make a buncha noise for a distraction so's the one behind the shack can sneak in and take the gal far, far away from here.

I looked over to Tor, "What do you think, Mr. Deputy?"

"I was thinkin' exactically what you is thinking." Tor grinned to make the statement a lie.

"Who does what?"

"Well, danged if you ain't the better shot and I'm the better injun. I'll get the gal and you get to shoot to your heart's content."

"My heart would be more content if I didn't have to ever shoot again. Specially, if I didn't have to kill again," I said it; meant it, too.

"If you kill a couple, they'll all dive for cover for sure. Just throwing lead isn't gonna put the fear of God into'em much."

"I know." I was not happy. "I'll shoot'em up right nice while you get the girl. I hope she's ugly and eight years old, and bites you when you grab her."

"If she is and does, I'll leave her there to chew on the crew down there. That could be why they have her guarded so well." Tor chuckled at his own wit.

"Bye. I'll meet ya where we camped two nights ago. Remember, her name is Diane."

Tor started off with his horse and the spare. "Diane the eight year old terror here I come."

"Howl like a coyote when you are in position."

"I can bark like one, but never howl," Tor just didn't sound too happy.

"Bark then. Daylight comes. Git."

I did all I could do at the moment, I sat back to wait and pray.

Tor led the horses to a gully heading in the right general direction. After a hundred yards he was out of sight of the shacks due to a rise coming between him and them. He climbed aboard the saddled horse and led the other at least a half mile beyond the shacks before he turned toward the back side of them. Thanks to another rise he was able to ride to within a few hundred feet behind the place he really wanted to be, the shack.

He dismounted and tied the horses off to some brush after he walked them until he could see the sparks fly from the fire. He crawled until he could see the target silhouetted by the fire behind it. Two men were in sight, one to the right of the shack and the other in back. The one in back stepped out into the light just like he knew there was someone who wanted to see him.

Tor crawled on his belly like a reptile until he was no more than a hundred feet behind the shack, rolled over on his back, cupped his hands around his mouth with the cone opening away from the ranch buildings, and let fly with his best imitation of a coyote barking.

I was near asleep when the sound of a barking coyote kicked me out of my dreams and wondered where it was. "Oh yeah. Time for some shoot'em up." I laid the barrel of my Winchester in the fork of a sage bush and lined up the sights on the man guarding the front of the shack. When I squeezed the trigger I knew it was a miss when the man was still standing there as the barrel came down and the sights were lined up again.

The man dropped like he was made of syrup, cold molasses syrup. He just folded in the middle and fell face first into the dirt. A moment later a cry went up and every man in sight moved toward anything he saw as cover.

I let fly with a shot. Another man tumbled to the left of the cabin. That left only the two dark sides guarded. The man that had been on the left side stepped into the light to find out what was going on and received a special delivery of lead just below his right collar bone.

Tor heard the first shot and saw the second man drop before moving toward the back of the shack, watching the man on the left side sneak his head out in the open. He drew his knife from the back of his belt and moved toward the man now kneeling at the right back corner of the shack. Shots were sounding all around the ranch area and all aimed up hill on the far side which he thought was a good idea.

The man guarding the back died with a second mouth gurgling blood directly under his chin. Tor moved to the other side. No one was there.

"Diane," he said in a calmer voice than he felt.

No answer.

"Diane." Much louder this time.

No answer.

He yelled, "Diane!"

15

"Hush up before you draw all them snakes around here," came from inside.

"You don't sound like you're only eight."

"What? I'm old enough. Get me out of here if you're friendly. Go away if you're not."

"I'm the cavalry comin' to the rescue."

"Then rescue and let's ride. My father's been hurt and I need to get to him."

"Your father has been taken care of. How do you think we knew you needed the cavalry?"

Right next to Tor's head a board snapped followed by a second. "Grab the boards and pull. This shack is just like the rest of this filthy snake pit, old and rotten."

Tor grabbed, pulling over and over again until he had an opening like a door for the voice to walk through. When she did he saw a slim build with a hat on top and heard spurs jingle at the bottom. "Come on." He grabbed a hand and started trotting toward the horses. The gal was pulling him within fifty feet.

They got to the horses, jumped aboard, and rode like they were worried a mite about the snakes coming after them.

I was caught up in the moment and continued to lay down a barrage until the Winchester clicked empty for the third time. The .44 came into my hand. I fired two shots and then loaded the rifle as slugs hit the dirt all around. "You can't even shoot," I yelled as the closest slug kicked up dirt over ten feet away. It dawned on me that dawn was coming to the world and soon I would be seen. Replacing the two rounds missing from the .44, I walked calmly to Solomon, swung into the saddle, and calmly rode straight away from the shooting down below.

Just as I reached the crest of the slope and was heading down the other side, two shots left the Winchester in the direction of the shacks with no thought of aiming. "Bye."

Long about noon, the sight of a rooster tail of dust off to the west was lit up by the sun. In moments I realized that the dust was being followed by dust. "Solomon, someone is being chased over there. We better check it out. Tor and Miss Diane might be in trouble."

I crossed the trail of tracks from their moving toward the Lazy E. The dust was coming straight for me. I moved off to the side of the trail to a group of rocks and scrub trees of some kind where I found a safe place for Solomon and a nest to set an ambush for the chasers.

Just as I laid the Winchester over a rock, a woman riding Tor's horse leading Tor on the pack horse and, from Tor's flopping back and forth, I could see he was hurt. No sooner had I figured that out eight riders topped the rise not a hundred yards behind. The woman was nice to look at even if she was dirty, sweating, and scared. I stood so she could see me and then squatted back down triggering two rounds toward the gun hands just as three of them decided it was time to shoot at the gal and Tor.

One man rolled off his horse under the hooves of the horses behind. The dance of the wounded man with the horses fascinated me. One horse hit the man and tumbled. Now there were two men and a horse involved in the dance. "Not a pretty sight even if it is interesting," I said to the rocks.

As the gal led Tor in behind a group of trees fifty feet past my position, I saw that Tor was covered in blood down his left side and the gal was on the edge of panic as she frantically jumped off her horse and tried to catch Tor as he fell off the wrong side of his horse. The deputy landed in the dirt with a plop like a watermelon dropped off a roof. The gal screamed and tried to get around the pack horse that was in a panic, rearing and screaming.

I looked back at the gun hands. They were still coming. None of them were firing their guns, all their targets had disappeared. As the six remaining riders slowed they spread out into a line like a cavalry charge. Behind a ways, one rider was running on the ground trying to catch up his limping horse and the second was sitting up in the dirt watching the blood run from his arm and trying to tie his bandanna around the wound. A man near the middle of the line became my target as I fingered the trigger. The man fell and five riders came straight at my little hidey hole firing as fast as they could.

I moved down so the long gun was situated between two rocks and the same two rocks provided a tremendous amount of cover.

Two shots brought down two more riders causing the other three to pull off into the trees up the slope from the trail. One man got up and staggered to a rock to hide behind while the other two just stayed still.

One man shouted, "You give us the woman and you can leave in one piece and upright."

"You go back and tell the boss that ain't gonna happen," was my reply.

"There's still three here to your one."

"There used to be eight. What's that tell you?"

"You got lucky from ambush, that's what." The man moved as he spoke.

Seeing the move, I splattered rocks all over the man. A few pieces of rock cut deep and drew blood. "I could have killed you, hombre, but I'm feelin' a bit generous. I don't know what you all had in mind for the young lady, but I'll find out and your boss will hear from me. I don't stand for a bunch of big strong growed up men picking on one woman alone. You ought to be ashamed."

The speaker for the ranch said, "Tell ya what. Let us ride outta here and we'll share your words with the boss. I will leave one man here to make sure you don't go nowhere until I get back." There was a laugh in his voice.

"Nope. You all will leave taking your wounded and dead, right now, or the buzzards and coyotes will feast tonight. I'll just have to kill the rest of you." I fired one shot and took the heel off the man's boot. It had been showing since the last move. "I coulda put that right next to the knife scar you have on your cheek, hombre. Now move or die. If you move this direction or stay you will die. I promise."

"Who are you? Why's your nose in none of your business?"

"Tor calls me 'The Deacon.' I'll be happy to say the service over your graves and read a few select passages from the Good Book. Now git!"

Silence reigned for about ten heartbeats.

"We'll leave." The man stood up in plain sight, turned, and went for his horse. He looked across the trail and yelled, "Come on, boys. Let's gather the horses and pick up our casualties and go back to see Everson. I ain't goin' against that gun over there for no amount of money. The boss is already behind in his paydays."

He climbed aboard his horse and trotted after two of their horses grazing back down the trail.

There was nothing for me to do but stay alert until they crossed the high spot. Then I rode to the high spot to watch them gather up another horse and keep on down the trail to the ranch. It was over.

I went back to where the girl and Tor had turned in.

Tor lay in the dirt with the girl working with pieces of Tor's shirt trying to stem the bleeding from his side. "Ma'am. Let me get on that. I've done it before."

"So have I." There was a definiteness in her voice. "Get me some water."

"Yes Ma'am."

I handed her a canteen.

"How'd he get hit."

"Lucky shot. Everson's gun fighters and rustlers were behind us a good two hundred yards when one of them up and pulls his Winchester out and lets one go in our direction. First shot. One shot. Zap it nails this man right through the ribs. Ain't no air bubbles, which is good."

"There is no exit wound either," I said.

"I see that. Nothing we need to worry about now. Who is he?"

"Man's name is Tor. He's a deputy city marshal outta Denver. We're on a fishing trip."

"And you are?"

"My name is Daniel Fount. Lately of Denver."

"Fount? You that preacher?" She smiled from a dirty face.

"Yup. That'd be me."

"Tor here told me we needed to ride and meet the Deacon."

"That's be me. He give me that name. I ain't likin' it much."

She turned back to the wound. I watched as her straw colored hair caught the slant of the rising sun's light. Having seen her eyes in the discussion and I was startled to see they were green, a deep pale green. "We buried your father right proper and went looking for you. Almost lost you after the rains. If it hadn't a been for a man in that little town, Black, we woulda never found ya."

She started as if stung by a bee. "Pa is dead. He told me that Pa had been taken care of and that's how you found out about me."

"We did take care of him. He was dying when I found him and talked a bit before he died. I found out you are Diane and someone named Everson owned a ranch and was givin' you trouble. He also said to watch out for someone or something that starts with 'Bur'."

"Bur?"

"Yep, he said 'kill Bur' and died."

"I know no Bur, or anyone whose name starts that way."

"It's a mystery we need to figure out. For right now let's get him on his horse with the saddle and move away from this spot. I'd rather not be here when the rest of the riders come back as I'm sure they must. This time they'll bring the boss."

"Everson is a killer and thief. He wants our ranch and is trying to force me to sign the deed over to him."

"Perhaps we can end his sin if he shows up. Where's a good place to defend with water, food, and a clear area for a battle ground?"

"The Rafter B. Our ranch. Oh, I guess it's my ranch now. Ma's been dead for three years. Typhoid got her."

We rode.

16

We spent another hour working at hiding tracks as we traveled just north of west. Much of my time was spent looking back from every high point. We came over a hump to find a small stream flowing in the opposite direction of our travel. Making a point of entering the stream at an angle up stream and then turned down stream once we were in the water.

"This riding in the water is losing time. It's just plain slow, and I don't like riding down in this little valley. No trees, no cover, anyone coming over that rim could see us a couple of miles away," I said in a low voice which sounded worried even to me.

Tor said, "It can work."

We were both surprised by his comment. He hadn't spoken before in this long ride.

"Welcome back."

"Find a rock shelf or gravel and get out of here."

We had passed just such a shelf a ways back. "Let's go back to that red rock shelf. You remember, the rock was so slick we almost dumped the horses."

"I remember."

I turned around and led the way.

The Rafter B did not have a large ranch house. The headquarters consisted of a house about thirty feet square, a steep roofed barn, a small bunkhouse, and a couple of other small sheds and shacks. The corrals were bull tight and well layed out. The main corrals were dog boned with two large areas out on the ends and a narrow runway between them. Off the runway were three or four small corrals. Lots of gates swinging in both directions allowed them to move and sort cows nice and easy with a minimum number of hands.

"Home sweet home," said Diane. "And, it's all mine. Only, I don't want it now."

"There's no way a woman could hold a ranch like this alone." I was looking around, "It is the best laid out place I've seen, but I haven't seen many."

We rode up to the house. Diane stepped off her horse onto the porch with practiced ease, dropping the reins at the horse's front feet. "You can stash the horses in the barn or the corral next to it. There's a door that'll allow the horses to go in and out. Should be feed in the barn unless some range rider used it all since we been gone. Ain't happened yet, but Pa was always worried it would happen when we left the place. I'll see if there's anything left to eat." She stepped through the front door.

I led Tor's horse to the bunkhouse and helped him down. Inside I laid him in a bunk on his good side and pulled the shirt bandages off slow and easy, using a knife to cut around the one spot that was stuck to the wound. "Wooowee. You got more black and blue than you got pink. Good news is that the bleeding has stopped and I can see a bump under a rib just around the corner on your back. Let's get some hot water and cut that slug out." I looked around. "Stove over there in the corner with a dutch oven on top. Be back in a few moments, don't go anywhere."

"Sure. I'll be right here for you to cut up like a side of beef."

"Naw. I won't do that. I just might carve the Lord's Prayer in your hide though."

A couple of old broken rails from the corrals and a match took care of the stove. Water from the well filled the dutch oven. An old shirt hanging on a nail made new bandages after they were boiled. Finding a whet stone in the barn next to the forge, I worked on Tor's knife a bit before announcing, "Okay, Mr. Deputy, it's time for the Right Reverend Daniel Fount to get rid of the sin in your body. I will deal with it one slice at a time. Bite this." I shoved a hunk of folded leather in the man's mouth as he opened it to speak.

I checked the lump again and with a quick move sliced a two inch gash over the slug.

"Man, leave a little there." Tor was not speaking softly.

I watched as the muscles in Tor's back convulsed.

The skin spread of its own accord and the slug rolled out onto the bunk.

Behind me came a sigh and then a thump on the floor. Diane just settling in a bunk on her side.

Shoving a piece of the shirt in the wound with one hand, I reached out to Diane with the other. That didn't work. Tor, who had lost enough blood already, got all my attention. Grabbing the needle and thread I had stuck in the post for just this purpose, I began sewing the wound just as I had watched a doctor do on my father's head one time in a small Kansas town after another brawl over a floosy.

Diane moaned.

Tor cussed.

Me? I finished sewing.

Hours later after a meal of pan bread from the kitchen and beans from a can we sat around the table and Diane stood at the wall. "I am not leaving this place. They will burn it and lay claim to it." Diane stomped her foot not once, but twice.

"How you gonna hold off twenty or more gundummies from Lazy E?"

"I don't know. But, I will tell you one thing, they won't take me alive. There's two men in that group that are going to die at my hand and that's a promise. They could not keep their hands off me and their hands were dirty. Filthy pigs! I'll kill them."

Tor's head came up staring at the table. "What?"

"Men like that should be shot down like dogs," Diane added as she stomped her foot, again.

I was not liking what was heard. Still torn between the image my father - phony that he was - had taught of the Christian that was always turning the other cheek, I was the man that knew what was going on here was wrong and could help do something about it. The Bible says for Christians to turn the other cheek and never states what you do after that second cheek was hit. It also says to take care of the widows and orphans. Here was an orphan and a woman alone all in one. What was I to do? I had asked that a lot lately and still was not getting a straight answer.

Of course, the fact that the orphan and woman was a very nice looking young lady all alone in a lonely patch of countryside did not have too much influence in the situation. "Ha ha," I said outloud.

"What?" Tor asked.

"Never mind. Just thinking."

"How can you laugh at me?"

"Diane, I am not laughing at you. I am laughing at the choice I need to make." I got up from the table and walked out into the darkness.

The moon had not risen. The stars were out providing more light than was necessary to go for a walk around the ranch buildings. Weren't nothing to do but look up in prayer. "Lord, you know what I am and all I am. I need your help. This gal needs your help. Tor needs your help. I am only one small man in your kingdom. Without you I am nothing. Guide me with Your wisdom and all the strength I need to keep this place safe. In Jesus' name. Amen."

My world went black.

The sun was two hands high in the sky when one eye opened. The ground the eye could see was dark dirt with a red tint. My head hurt like never before and there was the smell of smoke. Moving each leg one at a time and then each arm, I found one arm was tingling like it had been slept on wrong. I used the good arm to feel my head. There was a line plowed across the back of the only head I had and when the hand was checked there was blood, lots of blood.

"Okay, Daniel. You have been hit in the head, you are bleeding, and something is burning. Get up!"

After four tries I finally made it to my feet and was able to check out the surroundings. The house was in front of me looking like someone had kicked in the back door. "Backdoor? How'd I get here?"

I took two steps toward the back door and had to fight to get on my feet again. Entering the house, I saw it had been ransacked. Nothing was where it was supposed to be. The small secretary in the corner had everything dumped out of it and the drawers were smashed to kindling. The coffee on the stove was cold when I tried it.

I walked out front, the blood red cross of the gun butt felt good in my hand. "Was there a fight? Better check this .44." It was filled with five good rounds. I added the sixth.

Out the front door and across the yard to the bunkhouse I stumbled only to find it empty. My gear and Tor's were still in place on the top bunks. The bloody rags were still on the floor. The view from the door finally revealed the fire.

The shack furthest out was afire and almost completely gone.

The horses were not in the corral. I called, "Tor. Diane," as loud as I could muster which sounded like a dying frog. No reply.

Two buckets of water from the well dumped over my aching head cleared the vision and the mind enough that I was now sure the ranch had been attacked and the first one to go down was me. Someone dragged my carcass behind the ranch house from the middle of the yard and dumped it for dead. There was no sign of the girl or Tor.

"God. This is not the answer I was looking for," I said to the sky. In the house, I tried to find something to eat. A box of stale hardtack, if it's possible for hardtack to be stale, was all there was to eat. Flour was on the floor and any other basics I might use were gone. One can on the counter had a touch of brown sugar left in it which I dumped in my hand and licked between bites of hardtack broken up with the butt of a gun.

An idea hit as I crunched more hardtack. Solomon had come when I whistled before. Outside, I whistled as loud as I could and waited. Nothing.

The barn had nothing usable.

Absolutely nothing.

I walked back outside and there was Solomon walking down the slope behind the house. I whistled again. The horse lifted his head and ran. A filled well bucket satisfied the horse's thirst.

"Okay, Lord. I think you want me to be the Deacon that Tor talked about, kind of a protector of the widows and orphans. The question is how far do I go? It'd take a lot of killing to eliminate the evil men in this world that would prey on widows and orphans. Do I just kill them or only in self-defense?" The word 'defense' stuck in my mind. "So, just in self-defense it is. Thanks."

Twenty minutes later Solomon and I were on the trail of the riders leaving the ranch. Neither Tor nor the girl were anywhere on the ranch. I had even checked the ashes of the burnt building. The Winchester was fully loaded and a round was under the hammer, the sixgun held six rounds. Solomon seemed to sense the urgency of the situation and would put his head down every now and then, bring it up, and move a little faster.

"I think this horse is a blood hound and on the trail of one, or both of his old running mates."

Nobody answered.

A trickle of smoke eased through the boughs of the trees as I watched from a ridge line. The trees alongside a stream that reflected the sun like cheap glass beads an Indian might wear. I doubted the presence of an Indian. The trail led like an arrow to the smoke.

Just as I was set to go around and get ahead of them, they emerged from the cover of the trees and climbed the far side of the small valley. I could not make out a rider that looked like Tor, but the straw colored hair of Diane was a flag in the breeze. She was riding the pack horse with a saddle on it with her hands tied to the saddle horn.

All I could do was continue to follow, but first there was a short wait for them to clear the far side and that would give them back some of their lead.

Solomon got more and more antsy and ready to go. When Solomon could wait no more he whinnied and was answered from the trees. We watched the crowd going up the other side until they disappeared over the top before I turned Solomon loose and rode down to the campsite.

Tor was there and so was his horse.

The horse was lame. Tor was a mess. Blood oozed from cuts and holes all over his body. He was alive.

He smiled at me. "I'll see you in God's house. I told Him after I was caught that I was His to do with as He pleased. I asked for forgiveness from my doubts and sins, and I did plenty. Hey, I even named a few that I thought would keep me from Him. He took me in. I feel nothing. Through all this, I felt nothing. Well, Deacon, the task is all yours. I'm going away and will wait for you in Heaven. Do what you know you gotta do, my friend."

His head slumped and his entire body hung from the ropes he was tied with.

I cried like a baby. "This isn't what I asked for, either, Lord."

Tor's knife was stuck in the same tree he was tied to. I pulled it out, cut the ropes, and began doctoring the best friend a man could ever have. Most of the cuts were shallow and meant to bleed and cause pain. I walked down to the stream for water and washed his face when I returned. The cuts got washed. Two of them wanted to keep bleeding. Having nothing for a bandage, I worked up some clay and packed it over the wounds. Food came next.

Hunting was mighty poor at this time of day, but I prayed. Twenty minutes later a cow with a calf came out of the scrub to drink. It was never a good idea to be shooting calves, but this was an emergency. Kinda reminded me of Abraham sent to sacrifice his only son. God stopped him at the last minute and provided the sacrifice by having a ram caught in the bushes nearby. Maybe God provided this calf to save the life of Tor.

The beef steak was mighty good. After pounding the cooked meat with a rock against a rock it was tender enough for Tor to get some down. As I worked the steak for Tor, a dog came out of the woods and sat down near the fire. Not a particularly good looking dog, but big enough to scare me. He made no other move.

"Howdy."

The dog just looked at me, wagging his tail slowly.

"Hungry?"

Tail wagging increased and a line of drool eased out just back of his rather large canine teeth.

"Raw or cooked?"

I got the impression it didn't matter and tossed him a chunk.

It disappeared in no time at all. Again the dog sat wagging his tail slowly.

"More?"

An increase in speed and drool.

I cut off quite a bit of meat, a hind quarter, and tossed it his direction. He chomped down on it and drug it to the edge of the site where he proceeded to tear, chomp, and chew before swallowing one large chunk at a time.

The horse had a rock between the shoe and frog. I dug it out and walked the horse a bit after tightening the shoe, using a rock for a hammer on the nails. It wasn't a good fix, but it was a fix. Now I had two usable horses and a dog.

The Lord got some serious prayer sent His way along about then. I asked for everything from the life of my friend and Diane, to my safety, and a nice warm place to get some rest when it was all over.

Food was also mentioned in there. The dog's ears perked up at the mention of food.

I checked on Tor as he moaned and tried to move in his blanket. Where could I take him? He was in no shape to ride after Diane and the outlaws. Then I thought of the town where we dumped the bodies and had a reward waiting for us.

If my navigational skills were any good, that town was over the pass to the east maybe a total of a full day's ride. It would take me out of my way, but it would possibly save his life. Picturing the country, what little I knew of it, and then adding in a few terrain features that I could only hope were there, maybe, just maybe there would only be a day and a half or so of delay in reaching the Lazy E in time to save Diane.

I gave Tor the one night to rest up, and be doctored and babied, before putting him on his horse and starting for the pass.

We made it with Tor still alive. He wasn't conscious, but he was alive. The barber in the town, also the undertaker, said he would nurse my friend until he was able to travel and then send him on to Boulder. I gave him a chunk of the reward money to cover expenses and then left, praying.

Staring into the western sky as the sun set, I studied the problem laid out before me. There were twenty or more gun hands and outlaws down there. Diane was in the main shack with the fat man whom I assumed was Everson. The Bur that needed killing was somewhere, probably down there. There were two men at the front door and two men at the back. Men with rifles were positioned in pairs and one trio on high points all around the place. Six men, as near as I could determine, walked the grounds seemingly at random.

"Okay Lord. That's a bit much for me to tackle. What do you have in mind?"

All that came to mind was, 'walk in and get the girl.'

"We gotta be serious here, Lord."

I made sure no one was coming in my direction from any direction. The two men not a hundred yards away and uphill had not even looked my way. Everybody was watching the ranch yard like all the danger was down there. To the left was a shallow wash that would probably allow a belly crawl most of the way to the bottom of the hill, but from there to anything that could be called cover was a long way.

The dog had disappeared right after he finished that hindquarter and I hadn't seen hide nor hair of him since. I could use that dog long about now, but it just wasn't going to happen I figured. He was just a mooch and if I ever saw him again it would be when the food was on the table.

As the scene darkened, the cook hung his apron on the door to the cook shack. One man left the nearest lookout spot. I checked all around. Same thing was happening at all the points. The apron must have been a signal for the meal or watch change.

Without thinking, I stood up and walked straight for the cook shack. At the last minute I made a jog toward the house. With a hand covering the butt of the fancy Colt, I walked up to the back door guard on the house shack. "Wanna go eat. I got all I want of that swill."

"I'd rather not, but I gotta eat. Ain't had nothing since they cut up that man back on One Horn Creek. Rusty should be back in a minute or two. He don't like that food any more than you. I'm getting . . ." He walked away grumbling.

After giving a quick prayer of thanks, I opened the door.

The two barrels of a shotgun looked like train tunnels when they were pointed at my face. "Get back out where you belong. I told you men, no one comes in this house without my invite. Get."

It was the fat man.

"Yes Sir, thought I heard a struggle." I turned and walked out.

'Don't that beat all. I get right up to the man and he's got the drop.' Walking away from the back side of the house I saw a man moving in my direction. I dropped behind the ruins of the jail shack Diane had been in before. There was not much of it left standing. It looked like someone had a conniption fit and destroyed it. I laid there to see what was happening up close.

The man turned aside and knocked on the door. The fat man answered. They talked for a minute or two. The only words I caught were, "then someone else is in this area, find him," just before the door slammed in the man's face. The man ran to the front of the building shouting orders to everyone he passed.

Two men trotted around the house and set up station at the back door. Others went running everywhere, but no one thought of a tumbled down shack in plain sight. The lookouts were sent out to at least three more points and a couple of men were put on the roof of the bunkhouse, the highest perch on the site. The voice of the fat man shouted, "Take him alive and we'll teach him to leave us alone."

17

Surveying the area left few options. I could stay where I was or move and hope it would work out better. Just as I decided to stick until I could see really well, all havoc broke out. A man came running down the hill behind the house towing a horse. That horse was Solomon. It was definitely time to do something.

Then I saw the dog. He was traveling my direction a ways behind Solomon. He didn't look hungry; he looked like his pal was being taken away. That pal would be Solomon or the man dragging Solomon in.

The fat man came out of the house, listened for a moment, and started shouting orders about searching the place with a flour sifter if he had to, but he was getting the man who owned the horse. The fat man lined everyone up in two lines facing opposite directions. The lines were anchored on the house at one end and the bunkhouse at the other. The men were spaced just far enough away from each other that they could see each other and all that was between them.

He yelled, "Move straight ahead and comb every spot and pile and building on the place. I'll get the house and the area behind it. Hawkins, you get the area behind the bunkhouse."

"Yeah Boss," was the only reply.

I knew they would find my hidey hole in about 25 steps. I rolled sideways away from the building and found a dip I could not roll out of. Gathering my feet underneath me, I lunged and ran as fast as possible for the tree line a good quarter mile away. The dog was running beside me.

A man shouted, "There he goes," and someone threw a couple of quick shots into the night.

Let me tell you, I ran like a scared antelope covering ground faster than ever before, except maybe the time I got caught in the melon patch. I laughed as that thought went through my mind. The dog was just loping along like he was on a Sunday stroll. Shots were coming at a steady rate from behind, but nothing was hitting very close. The sound of men running soon disappeared in the sound of horses running.

I stopped and turned, gun in hand. The dog kept going.

Six horses were just passing the running men. Only three of the horses had riders, allowing the runners to attempt to catch and mount the free running horses. I watched as one man swung into the saddle by grabbing the horn and then sailed all the way over the horse making a hard landing the dirt face first.

I fired two shots, turned and ran. Shots hit the dirt where I had been standing. In moments I saw a shallow ditch to the left and angled for it. It was too shallow for much of anything, let alone cover. The trees were closer, but still out there a ways. At the edge of the trees sat the dog.

The poofs of dust were getting closer. I saw the sky line and realized I was running over a hump. The stars ahead of me made a great target for the outlaws to have. Cutting back to the right, I willed myself to go faster and prayed deep in my head. 'Lord, this is a bit more delivering than I had asked for. If I had another choice, I'd ask for them to all fall down and let me get to the trees.' I looked back.

They were still coming.

I stopped, turned, and let fly with two more rounds. The rider fell off the lead horse. Then I ran what I thought was faster still. 'This ain't getting no easier, Lord. I know You said that vengeance belonged to You in Your book. So, you wanna take Your vengeance on these sinners, please? Any time now would be fine.'

Somewhere I found more energy and kicked my feet out in front a bit further with each stride. Before I really thought about what to do next, trees were passing by. A sharp turn to the left seemed appropriate. I saw the ditch just in time to jump it and got a great idea from it.

A large tree 50 yards further became a barricade. I turned. Punched out the fired rounds and poked 4 rounds in as replacements. Looking back, I could see three riders entering the trees. They would go on past if they continued that direction and I would be covered on two sides. Not a good position when a man is afoot and the chasers are on horses.

I fired three shots directly at the lead man who fell forward over the neck of his horse. As the wounded man hung on, the other two drew up. I fired one more round which hit nothing but the air it passed through as far as I could tell, but it had the desired effect. The two riders turned to charge my position and ran their horses into the ditch.

I ran back and with a heavy hand smacked both men with the barrel of the .44. They both ended on the dirt in disorganized piles. The horses both had broken legs and were shot. I quickly reloaded. "One of them could have come through this with four good legs, Lord. I would be riding now, but thanks anyway. You're in charge and not me. Where to now?"

All I heard was, 'Whistle.'

I whistled.

Working a way through the trees further away from the runners, I was ready to fall down and take a rest. The sound of horse's hooves coming from the direction of the ranch made me stand up and shout. The sky was beginning to look a bit gray allowing a bit better sight in the thickly wooded area. The way out was going to be too well lit in a matter of minutes and would leave no chance against the riders coming except for Solomon.

A whinny sounded.

"Solomon?"

Another whinny.

"Solomon. Here boy, you good looking devil you."

The horse extended his muzzle; it got a quick pat before I swung into the saddle. My spurs just naturally gigged the horse's ribs giving the horse direction. The horse lit a shuck outta there, swerving right and left through the trees at a clip that caused the rider, me, to lie down on his neck and pray the horse was the better tree dodger.

When there were no more trees whizzing by, the sky was light enough for even a human to see the trees in spite of the forest. There was just one problem, there were no trees and we were running horse's belly to the ground across a large open flat area.

Shots sounded behind me. I turned. They were far away and off their horses trying for a lucky rifle shot. Nothing landed anywhere near.

I eased back on the reins and said, "Easy there, big boy, we got a ways to go and there may be more coming." I was checking the surroundings as I spoke; the hills to the right looked like the best option.

'It's going to be a long ride around the Lazy E in order to get in position again so I can save that gal,' I was thinking.

We rode it, Solomon and me, taking over six hours of dodging riders and finding ways over and around the terrain.

Not a soul stirred on the grounds of the Lazy E as we stood in the middle of the yard that had bristled with men six hours before. The .44 hung in a limp hand as I looked around. Tracks covered the ground showing a lot of moving around and also told the story of a rapid evacuation of the grounds.

Why?

Where to?

Where's the girl?

I entered the last building to search, the house shack. The stench of old sweaty men's bodies was heavy. I checked the only other room to find a bed, if you want to call it that, covered in a tick mattress that was more lump than mattress. No woman's things were left out in the open that could be seen right off. A shiny object caught my eye. I picked it up, a concha; a concha from the belt the girl had been wearing.

Into my vest pocket it went as a smile grew on my face. I left the ranch site with a new zeal to get that gal out of the hands of the Lazy E. Anyone smart enough to leave clues like that was someone I wanted to rescue and get to know much better.

After riding a mile straight away from the buildings, we, me and Solomon did a circle all the way around. Tracks showed that the men leaving had left in groups of two and three, all going in different directions. "That ain't gonna work, boys. All I gotta do is follow one of you and I get to the meet up spot. The question I have is which one of you has Diane with you?"

I started following each set of tracks leaving the ranch one at a time. On the third one just hundred yards or so from the house was another concha. It matched the one already in my vest pocket. I pointed Solomon's nose along the direction of the tracks and kicked Solomon into a steady, ground eating gallop.

Within two hours it was easy to tell that Solomon was about done in. I saw a small trickle of water coming from a seep into a water-carved basin just a dozen feet off the trail and stopped. "Not the best place to camp, but it works."

The horse nudged the water and sucked what was in the basin, which wasn't much, and then walked toward some dried grass still standing beyond the seep. From the strength of the trickle of water, it was going to be an hour or so before the basin would be filled again and I could get a drink. Both horse and rider settled in for a nap.

We had not gone very far after resuming the tracking, when the revelation popped into my head. The three horses that made the tracks were headed for the gal's ranch. "Wish I knew the country. It'd be nice to swing around and beat them there."

Not a mile more, Solomon stopped. I looked around for a reason and tried to get him to keep on the trail which was pointed at a group of mixed aspen and fir on the far side of an open area. Every time I would pull his head around, the horse would turn to the right. I finally let him go the way he wanted which was the downwind side of the grassy meadow. I wanted to get across the meadow and this was just the long way.

Not but a few moments into the circle, the strong smell of smoke filled the air. "Is that a camp or a rest spot, Solomon?"

The horse bobbed his head.

We travelled on until I caught the hint from the horse that it was time to turn back to the trail which brought us to a spot where the fire and the movement of men around the fire were seen. "Looks like they're in for the night. Got'em a brush shelter, for the lady of course, and a chunk of something on the fire. All set up nice and comfy like. A man was hunkered down near the fire pouring something into a cup from a rusty bucket."

I dismounted and started toward the fire. That dog showed up on my right. 'Where'd you come from dog?' I thought.

Half way to the fire there was a noise off to the right. As I turned swiftly in that direction, my world went crazy. A dizziness hit, my eyes refused to focus, and the day went dark as I fell to the dirt.

I woke up to the sun on the other side of the sky. I had been out all night. Trying to stand was a comedy show in itself. Where was the dog? A whistle brought the horse after I checked in the direction of the fire to find nothing there. The horse walked up behind as I was checking the .44. I turned quickly and the dizziness hit again, only this time there was a tree to grab and hold on to and regain total consciousness at the same time. Solomon looked at me as if to agree we had a problem.

I took inventory. I had been shot in the back of the head. I had fallen a few times. I had not eaten for two days. The combination had not come together for good in my head. Cogitating on all of it brought back a memory of a time when Evelyn had been climbing the steps into the caravan just as my father had opened the door in a powerful hurry, catching Evelyn in the head. Evelyn had gone down hard, landing on the back of her head. She was dizzy and out of sorts for a few days. Dad was mad because she could not sing and draw the crowd. He weren't worth spit as a singer, although he was genuine when he tried.

Dad had called her problem something or other, the name of which was hanging on the back of my mind. A concussion. That's what the problem was, a concussion. How long would it last? How many times would I fall? How was I going to rescue the gal if I kept sleeping for many hours at a time? Something about sleep rang a bell. Someone with a concussion was not supposed to go to sleep for a day or so.

Well, I had stayed awake for a couple of days so I should be more than all right. But, I was not all right. Why?

"Solomon, we got a problem." The horse bobbed his head.

"Is that the only answer you have?" The horse bobbed his head.

"Forget it." The horse bobbed his head.

I took the reins and walked into the campsite. Another Concha was lying in the dirt just under the edge of an emerging fiddle neck fern. Next to it was the 'Rafter B' brand scratched in the dirt with an arrow.

I had been right, if I could have reached I would have patted myself on the back. Now all that was left to do was get there. Something else caught my eye. On the fern curl was a spot of what looked like blood. Her blood? Was she trying to show that she was hurt or being hurt?

"Come on, Sol, we got places to go, people to see, and no time to get there."

I let the horse set the pace with a little judicious spurring.

18

The Rafter B was quiet, way too quiet. Horses stood in the corral, a couple tied at the hitch rail with saddles on over by the bunkhouse, and one rider way off to the other side headed in. From the horse count, there were at least 22 men on hand to keep the party lively and me on my toes. As I watched from the same point Tor and I had used before, I prayed. It was a simple prayer, "Lord, help me please."

I didn't know what else to say.

The dog hadn't been around for some time, at least not since I fell asleep in the dirt. No worry, sometimes I think that dog is an angel from God and other times he hits me like a demonic spirit. I could have used that dog right then. His smile and tail talked louder than most words.

As I watched, one man walked from the bunkhouse over to the barn. In a couple of minutes I could hear the bellows pumping in the forge and saw smoke come from the chimney. That gave me the location of two of the men. The front door on the house opened and out stepped Diane. She was looking back over her shoulder like someone was giving her instructions.

She flipped her hair by throwing her head around and walked to a swing chair. Her standing there was doing things to me. She had obviously had a chance to clean up and change clothes. There was no sign of any bruises that I could see from this distance. She sat and started rocking back and forth with one foot while she tucked the other underneath her. As she rocked she kept throwing her hair. I got the feeling she was trying to say something to anyone watching. She knew it would have to be me because no one else knew she was a captive and her father was dead. Except the outlaws that is.

'What could she be trying to say, Lord?'

The flip was always in the same direction, to her right. Every time she did the flip her hair would fall over the right side of her head and promptly slide back to the left. What was she saying, if she was saying anything?

She lifted her right hand and arm so the arm rested on top of the swing back. She knocked on the wood a couple of times and then slowly extended her pointer finger and brought the hand to a quiet position with that finger pointed.

Okay, so there was something over that way that was important. The sun was over there and a couple of hours from setting. I was sure she was not pointing at the sunset. There were no colors painted, yet.

I tried to focus on the area to the west from her angle. There was nothing but wide open spaces, or so it looked from where I was. Then I saw the dog. He was sitting very still about two hundred yards out from the side of the house to her right. Anyone not knowing what that dog looked like would only see a scrubby bush if he could see anything looking into the sun like that.

Had she given something to the dog to give me if I showed up? Was it her dog? Questions I had no answers for at that time. One thing was sure, I was going to move around and join that dog about sundown.

After a few minutes she talked with someone inside the house, stood up, stretched like she was tired and going to bed, turned, and walked into the house with her left arm slapping the wall beside the door jamb three quick times with her knuckles. Three raps. Three shots. Danger or trouble. Most of the time it was the signal for 'I need help.' Was that what she was doing?

An answer slapped the back of my mind. She needs help to get to the dog or that way. Wait, she signaled she is going to bed for the night at a really early, too early for a young gal. She is going to sneak out of the bedroom on that side of the house and go in that direction and will need help. She's that sure that I am out here somewhere.

'Lord, you and I know she needs all the help she can get.'

I started sliding backwards toward Solomon. Once I reached him, we walked slowly, very slowly so we kicked up no dust, away from the house until it was relatively safe to mount up and head west.

The darkness took a long time coming that evening.

When it did, Solomon and I headed for the dog.

There was no dog.

I could see the light of a lamp through the front room window. The window on the same side, but further back on the house was opened half way and dark. I watched standing in front of Solomon just in case someone saw us from the ranch. With the two merged figures a watcher would see neither horse nor man, instead it would be some object like an old tree or something strange.

A dark figure eased out of the back window of the house to the ground. It was easy to see the dark against the white wash on the wall. I figured it was her and watched her move to the back corner of the house before dropping to hands and knees, crawling toward me ever so slowly.

The bunkhouse door swung open and one of the hands stepped out for an after dinner smoke. I had never seen them eat dinner.

A figure moved at the front room window. The fat man stepped to the window and looked out.

He knew she was leaving. He knew sooner or later I would show up. The hands were staying undercover so I would not be scared off by their movements or presence. This was all just one big trap to catch whoever was after the girl, and that would be me.

Diane was so confident of her escape, through the open window that the fat man had left open on purpose, that she stood and walked rapidly all hunched over. Her in those dark clothes were going to be very hard to see from the house or the bunkhouse as she got further and further away from the house and other buildings.

I was cheering inside with, 'Go Diane, go!'

She was coming right at me like she could see me.

I moved off her path a good fifty feet and covered Solomon's muzzle so he would not make a noise.

The bunkhouse door opened again and two men stepped out. They gathered two sets of reins from the horses tied there and swung into the saddles before riding to parallel her path. The outlaw in the barn came out on horseback and paralleled her on the other side. The fat man moved out to the porch and took up position sitting in the swing. He obviously planned on holding court for my hanging from that position after his boys caught me and drug Diane back.

So, he still did not have her signature on the deed that he needed, was my first thought. My second was he would kill her this time and forge a signature or make up a very large story to cover his occupying the Rafter B. A third thought was that he could burn the barn with the two of us in the ashes and no one would be the wiser when he told folks he bought the place from her just before the accident.

Tor and I were the only ones that knew where her father's body was and Tor was not going to be available.

I was in the fat man's way as much as the gal.

'Lord, I need Your help.'

19

As Diane came abreast of me I said, "Keep walking. You're being followed. Don't worry, I'll meet up with you."

She started a bit, but kept it calm. "Please hurry. I just know they're gonna kill me soon."

"Did you sign the deed over?"

"No."

"Keep walking."

I turned to check on the followers. The single rider was coming straight at me and the other two were out of sight in the dark and probably behind a rise in the land. Diane kept in going without changing pace.

There was a rope on my saddle, but I had never roped anything in my life. Even when the other boys were roping hay bales and fence posts, I sat and watched. Dad raised me to be a phony preacher just like him. I really fooled him, didn't I?

As the single rider came on I moved toward him going from one tree to another until I was in a great position. He saw my horse and got real cautious, climbing down off his horse, and creeping forward.

As he passed my position, I clubbed him on the back of the head with my .44. He fell like he was dead.

I rode to intercept the other two riders, leading the horse I had just liberated from its rider.

By the time I caught up with Diane she was out of the woods and moving quickly across an open grassy plain. Dark spots shaped like cows dotted the country side and a clump of what appeared to be trees could be seen in the distance. I decided the best thing to do was just ride up to her, get her on the horse, and escort her on her way. The two gundummies could follow or attack, I really did not care.

Matter of fact, I was getting some angry over this whole situation. The greed of the fat man, Everson, and the lack of respect by his outlaw bunch, just plain burned me. Every list of things that God hates starts with pride and if you check those lists, pride is a piece of everything on the list. 'Lord, give me the wisdom to deal with all this, including the challenges to my ignorance of Your desires.'

We talked quietly a bit as we rode. Out of the corner of my eye I watched for the riders off to the left and could not tell them from cows or elk in the grass. There were just dark shapes here and there. All I could think of was they were snakes in the grass and just as difficult to see.

We arrived at the trees which surrounded a spring filled small pond where the cows had left their sign of many visits in the past. "You keep on riding and I'll see what I can do about them two." I nodded in their direction.

The dog appeared out of nowhere and stayed with the woman as they rode off. Was he her dog?

Two dark spots turned to come straight at us as the distance between the two of them widened. I said a quick prayer under my breath and settled in to a great spot behind a tangle of tree trunks and scrub brush, and waited.

The first one to catch sight of me had his sixgun in hand and would not have seen me if I hadn't said, "Surrender." He started to raise the pistol, so I shot him out of the saddle. As I fired, I heard a shot behind me and felt a round graze my left arm like a hot iron. I turned to see a dark shadow bringing his sights to take another shot at me. He didn't like it that I did not fall down and die with his first shot. His second shot missed. He needed some practice. I decided he wasn't going to get any practice, I shot him out of the saddle. He fired at the sky as he fell. He finally hit what he was aiming at.

I rode like my horse's tail was on fire to catch up with Diane. "Let's ride."

She kicked her horse into a run alongside me. We covered some ground for about ten minutes when I called, "Let's ease'em down to a gallop and head toward the east and the mountains. We need some cover." The dog was still alongside her.

Morning found us snuggled into a clump of rocks in the foothills with a small, very small fire keeping us warm. As soon as I could make out separate rocks a hundred feet away, I saddled the horses, woke Diane, and we left the place. Swinging up into the saddle had caused my head to swim and I had to hold on with both hands to keep from falling. That wasn't good at a time like this.

"You know how to get outta here to some civilization where we can find help and a bit of rest?"

"I think so."

"You lead, I'll follow."

As we rode I told her my problem. The look of fear on her face scared me.

"Just keep going if I go down. You won't be able to put me on a horse, so you get to safety. If you can hide me a bit, that would be good, but don't leave my horse with me. Take him down the trail a mile or so, and let him go."

"What do I do then?" she asked.

We discussed that issue for a bit, until she went silent. I dropped back further.

It was dark, very dark. I was on the ground and it was cold. A blanket was over me, my head throbbed, and it was dark. Trying to stand was a failure for the first two times. I was able to stand only if I held on to something solid, like the tree next to my blanket. "Diane," I whispered.

No reply.

"Diane," I said in a normal voice, except there was a twinge of fear that I didn't like in the sound of it.

No answer.

Moving from tree to tree, I got to the horses. Actually, it was just horse, Solomon. Diane's horse was gone and so was her saddle. Why had she left alone? Why was I on the ground? Why was it dark when it should be early?

I had to think hard through the pain to come back to the answer, my concussion. I had blacked out and she did what I told her. She left me. She left me covered with a blanket and Solomon. For both I had to thank her. My Winchester was gone.

I checked the saddle bags, but found nothing there to eat. We hadn't had anything to eat in a day before I blacked out again, and now I was going to have to look for her tracks, find food, and catch up to her before the Lazy E crowd, specially the fat man. Not a goal I was too sure I could handle.

A sharp noise rattled through the woods. I drew the .44 and stood as silent as the rock next to me. Solomon's head came up. I grabbed his muzzle to keep him silent. We waited.

Another horse? No.

Must be a person making that much noise. No.

It was a cow, a big ugly fat cow, also referred to as beef steak on the hoof. If I shot the poor dumb critter I might as well send a telegram to the ones following us and tell them where to meet me.

The cow got to live a bit longer. I slowly and carefully saddled Solomon, eased myself into the saddle, and started to go . . . where? I had no idea. I checked the big dipper. A couple of hours left until it would begin to get light. I slowly climbed down and, leaning against a rock and wrapped in my blanket, I waited for enough light to see her tracks.

I woke again with the sun just over the horizon. Solomon was still saddled and not very happy with me. He nudged me and gave out with a couple of grunts as if to say, 'Let's go, laggard.' I really couldn't blame him.

The tracks of a fast moving horse left that campsite heading east. It had to be the tracks of Diane's horse. We took out after them.

In the morning light the tracks were easy to follow. If they were easy for me, I knew they'd be easy for any real hand on a ranch. For a while I drug a bush along behind, but looking back all I'd done is make an easier track to see the trail.

There was about three miles behind me when the sound of a rifle shot came from up ahead. Solomon kicked the speed up a bit and we went running into battle.

The sound of a couple of sixguns going off echoed off the steep sides of a valley we were entering. We splashed through a small stream and up the other bank, still on the tracks. The problem became very evident. Two other sets of tracks joined Diane's. She was in trouble.

The rifle sounded again, followed by a sixgun.

I was behind two chasers which were between Diane and me. I couldn't shoot until I knew the positions of both Diane and the two outlaws, or at least I was assuming they were from the Lazy E. Another pistol shot, this time closer.

I left the saddle and tried to walk, leading Solomon. That didn't work. My head began to swim and I went down.

The sun had moved about two hours' worth when I woke up. I wasn't as confused as earlier, but there was still the problem of getting into the saddle. When I finally did, I was seeing double and Solomon wanted to move. We moved at whatever speed Solomon wanted to go and all I did was hang on.

At least there were no more gun shots.

For awhile.

Not two miles down the path, four more horses joined the three I was tracking. Now there were six outlaws on the trail of one young gal that just wanted to see her father buried proper and get her ranch back. The more I thought on that idea, the madder I got. Why? Why was this outlaw rancher so intent on gaining a ranch that he would kill her father and then go after a woman in a time and place where woman were looked upon as more holy than any church. You could burn down every church in the state and just rile folks a bit, but mess with a woman and every man jack of them would be on your trail with a hanging rope over the horn.

At this point, Everson had to kill her and bury her deep. If she made it to a real town, he would be a hunted man and so would all his hands, or gang. I was already on his trail and I intended to be the one who read to him from the Good Book and told him of his sins. God could deal with him when the time came for his final judgment. I didn't want to be judge, jury, and executioner. I just wanted the girl safe and sound in her own home.

I looked to the heavens and said, calmly, "Is that too much to ask, Lord?"

Thunder rolled through the new canyon Solomon had just taken the two of us into.

I didn't like the sound of that answer.

Solomon moved on like he knew what he was doing and I just worked at staying in the saddle and making sense of the sights I was seeing double. No more shots rolled through the canyon as the walls got steeper and the stream ran faster.

I heard a shout.

Solomon stopped before I could pull back on the reins. I slowly swung my right foot over Solomon's rump and eased myself to the ground. Taking my left foot out of the stirrup was no easy task, but Solomon stood for it. I dropped my end of the reins in the dirt just in time to see the dog moving through the boulders on the other side of the stream. Where had he been? I didn't really care, I was just glad to see him. I whistled softly and he ignored me. I moved parallel to the dog as we moved up the trail alongside the stream.

Another voice said, "Catch up when you can. I ain't missing the fun when they catch that gal."

"Some pard you are, Doby."

I listened to hear Doby ride away followed by the other man grumbling about a busted latigo way out here in the middle of nowhere.

The trail went up steeply alongside a ten foot tall water fall. Kinda pretty it was, but who had time to appreciate the creation around them in times like this. My head came slowly over the top at the edge of the falls to see a man fumbling with his saddle, which lay in the dirt. He was trying to piece together two pieces of broken leather.

It looked to me like the mice had gotten to his latigo and done a right smart job of eating a fair sized chunk out of the strap. Only two ways I knew to fix that; rivets or a new strap. He tried to use just the ring end of the latigo only to find it too short to make a tie. He reached in his saddle bag and pulled out a strip of leather, a short half-inch wide and thick about three feet long. Using his knife he cut the two chewed ends of the latigo off square and over laid them. The pocket knife he dug out of his ducking trousers had a long, narrow blade which he used to start a hole through the two ends of the latigo.

I could see what he was planning on and filed that idea in the back of my mind should I ever need it. He was going to sew that latigo together with the leather. He tossed the leather strip in a backwater of the stream and as he did caught sight of me. He grabbed for his gun.

I hauled mine out, but before I could get it over the edge of the trail, the dog came running and leaping across the stream to land in the middle of one surprised gun hand whose gun went flying and feet went out from under. The dog stood on his chest and growled in his face. I stepped up and took the knives away from the outlaw. The big knife I had to roll him a bit for, but the pocket knife was lying in the dirt next to him.

The dog backed off when I asked him to.

"Stand up and tell me the name of the man I'm gonna bury right here."

"You ain't burying me."

The dog didn't like the sound of his voice or something, he took the man down again.

The man's hand flashed into his shirt and came out with a short barreled small caliber pistol which I heard click twice as he thumbed the hammer back. I didn't think. I just shot the man as he laid there trying to get that barrel lined up with me or the dog.

The dog backed off and wagged his tail. Last I saw of him he was going over the next rise on the trail while I was gathering what I could use of the man's rig. Two chunks of jerky were a blessing and that little, short barreled pistol, and his gun belt were going to come in handy I was sure.

As I rolled him off the trail, I was quoting the Good Book to him for a service.

Now there were only five after Diane.

20

The double vision was going away. I could move without getting dizzy. Getting on Solomon was not the task it had been just moments ago. "You fixin' me up, Lord? I give You thanks for that."

We moved slowly up the trail figuring someone would come back to check on the man left behind, but no one did after a half hour. Solomon slowly picked up the pace until we came to a place where someone, Diane probably, had rolled a rock and caused a slide to cover the trail with large rocks and also dam up the stream.

The Lazy E boys had moved enough rock to get their horses over the blockage making a spillway for the pool backed up by the rocks and a new chunk of trail which I promptly used and moved on at the tail end of the parade.

As I rode I was looking at the tracks. There were three I could identify anywhere due to some weird markings, but the others all looked the same to me. I was trying to figure out which one was Diane's, but had no luck by the time the sun was low in the western sky. With about an hour to find a secure place to camp, the trail split. The tracks of the horses went one way on a Y in the trail, which was cresting the pass not more than two hundred yards ahead. The creek was down to almost no water in it being this close to the top. I could even see where the trickle began near a pair of rocks not fifty feet ahead.

I filled my canteen and took the other way at the Y until I was sure no one was following and began looking for a camp spot. My figuring was that I would set up a camp and walk up to the pass after dark and see what I could see of a campfire close by, or even cabins or a town in the distance. We were high enough up that unless the view was blocked by more mountains, the view should be long and informative.

Maybe a quarter mile up the side path, I found a spot. Just as I was swinging off the back of Solomon, I noticed as single small boot track in the dirt right where I figured to put my bed. It was a flat spot maybe six feet wide and protected on two sides by rocks three feet high. The track looked to have been made by someone going from rock to rock, but there they had to hit the dirt because the jump was too far.

Eyeballing the direction the boot was pointing, I took out to see if any more tracks showed up. The reason was simple. I was sure this was a track of one of the boots Diane was wearing. Diane had sent her horse down one trail as she got off and headed down the other going from rock to rock alongside the trail. Those gundummies would never think of a trick like that. Why would anyone leave a perfectly good horse to walk on top of rocks when there was no way they could get back to the horse? And, it looked like it was a long way to anything down this new trail.

Me, I just walked Solomon until I found another track closer to the trail and kept on going. I started singing 'Amazing Grace' as I rode along hoping to catch up before it was so dark there was a chance of missing her if she turned off.

"Who taught you to sing, cowboy?"

"My daddy's star attraction," was my answer.

"Got room on that horse for me?" She stood up right next to the trail not fifteen feet in front of me. The dog was at her side.

"Where'd the dog come from?"

"He's been around off and on all day. Is he yours?"

I chuckled, "No. He belongs to Him. No one is that dog's master, unless he's a hound from heaven and belongs to God."

"Probably. Oh, it is good to see you up and about."

"I'm feeling better, but I ain't all the way there yet." I stuck my hand out and down slightly, "Grab on and let's get a bit further down the road before it's totally dark."

She did and we loped along watching for something on our back trail and a place we could fort up and get some rest for the night. Just after it got really black, we crawled into a shallow cave. A rock wall about a third fallen, stretched across the mouth of the cave leaving an opening large enough for Solomon to get in. He refused the shelter and went out to dinner with the dog. The dog loved the place. I let Diane take the first watch at the rock wall to the front of the cave and I got some shuteye.

I awakened to a low growl from the dog. He was looking back up the trail and just rumbling under his breath. Diane was sound asleep leaning against the wall. Solomon was standing next to his saddle.

We saddled in record time. I put Diane aboard Solomon and, leading the horse, I trotted down the trail. The dog disappeared so fast he might as well been a poof of smoke.

That running stuff is for the birds in or out of boots and I was wearing high heeled riding boots. After a mile, I sent Diane on ahead with the horse and I took the rifle to set up a watch on the back trail. She got the small sixgun. I didn't think to give her extra shells for the gun.

After almost falling asleep in the first five minutes I was hunkered down to watch, I stood up. When I did a slug whanged off the rock right next to my head. The sound of a shot followed as I slid back down into my hidey hole. Taking a quick peek to see what I could see, I saw nothing. Someone else did. Another round went splat into the same rock. Either the first shooter moved or there was more than one. I went with two shooters.

I prayed.

I prayed for that silly dog to show up and for Diane's safety.

Thinking on what I had seen of the terrain before I hunkered down and knew they could not get past me without me knowing it or being dead of course. I was watching for the first and didn't want to think about the second.

One man popped up and right back down just like a prairie dog after a long winter's sleep. I didn't move. He tried it again. I didn't move. The third time he lost his senses, I killed him with a bullet through his head.

The second and third and then fourth outlaw returned fire. I was getting a lot of attention and they were some angry because I had killed number one. I crawled behind rocks to a second spot off twenty feet or so.

The new spot did give them a route to get by me without me seeing them, but I doubted if they could see it from their angle. The way they had followed us and not cut us off told me they didn't know this area any more than I did and who would find anything in the jumble of rocks unless they stumbled on it like I did.

While I was trying to make up my mind what to do next, the sound of four or five shots rattled off the mountains from the direction Diane had gone. It was time to go.

I flung three shots in the general directions of the outlaws and started around the corner of trail behind me. Once I was clear it was back to running again. Those gundummies were sure trying to murder those rocks back yonder where I left from. They must have fired off at least a box of shells. I smiled. I wasn't there.

The trail went uphill for a short distance and then topped out in a nice campsite situated in the saddle. A problem became very, very clear. Going down that other side I would be in plain sight for at least five minutes even if I ran. There weren't nothing else to do if I wanted to get Diane out of her predicament.

The trail went zigzag down the mountain with one level not twenty feet above the next. Every time I was going across I was like a shooting gallery I saw in St. Louis once with a bunch of ducks moving across the scene and the object was to shoot them down as fast as they popped up. I never got to try that, but my dad did and didn't do very well. He could hit a target standing still, but he couldn't hit the slow moving ducks that were larger than the bullseye he could hit standing still. I was hoping the men behind me were as bad as my dad.

They weren't. The first one to shoot took a chunk out of my rifle's butt leaving splinters hanging out for me to poke in my face when I brought the Winchester up to return fire. When I got to the next switchback I just kept on going straight ahead. There was a stream at the bottom of the hill, but it was a long way down there.

After I travelled most of the way downhill on the slope, someone saw me and fired a couple shots that sent twigs and needles falling on my head. I turned straight down the hill and did fairly well until I was fifty feet or so above the stream where I tripped and pretended to be a tumbling act in a circus all the way to the water, where we, the water and I, met with no introduction, just a noisy, wet connection. The rifle was still in my hand when I came up for air.

The dog was sitting on the bank.

I reached for him and he took off downstream along a hard rock ledge and disappeared around a rocky corner. He was trying to tell me something, of that I was sure. The trail got a washing as I trotted in his steps shaking the water out of the Winchester and my .44. In no time at all I rounded another corner and ran into Solomon. Solomon without Diane. He had a bleeding spot on his hip that I checked. It was a grazing shot that probably hurt more that it was dangerous.

He actually looked like he was happy to see me. I know I was happy to see him. Matter of fact, you could say I was overjoyed.

21

My position in the saddle gave me even more confidence that God was looking out for me. I yelled, "Thank ya, Lord," and kicked Solomon into a fast walk. It was a gentle kick.

Down the trail we found a spot where the ground was all torn up. Must have been the place where the shots I had heard were fired. Three fired rounds lay in the dirt and a piece of wet plaid cloth that matched the shirt Diane had on was lying atop a rock like someone had put it there on purpose. More trail markers from Diane? I wasn't sure of this one.

The dog barked from downstream. We took off after him. This time I gave Solomon his head and let him go his own speed which, due to the narrow trail, wasn't very fast, but it was dangerous for me, the rider, as limbs whipped and a couple were the size that wouldn't bend for nothing. I had to duck, quickly. Horse tracks with dog prints over the top of them filled the trail. I could smell fresh dust. Another piece of shirt was hooked on a branch to the high side of the trail.

It was her.

I gigged Solomon telling him to move faster. He held to the pace he had. I let him, he was smarter about the trail than me.

We splashed through the stream and up the other side a bit before going down and across the stream again. After six or seven crossings, I could tell by the water splashed on the bank still soaking in that we were catching up. I pulled back on the reins, not wanting to run into them when they had the advantage and I wasn't ready. Of course, I really didn't think I was ready for any of this. It was a good thing I slowed us down.

Around the next corner there they were, just crossing the creek again into a tangle of aspen and scrub. The one at the back jumped off his horse and unlimbered his long gun. He was pretty good. From about 200 yards, he planted that slug in the tree right next to my head. I mean not even a foot away. Needless to say, I hit the dirt, digging as I landed.

From a distance came the shout of victory from the shooter. He was sure I was down and yelled he was coming to get my scalp. Someone else told him to come back, but he kept coming.

I could have, but I didn't take his scalp. He was dead from a gunshot wound when I left him.

I didn't shoot him, it was the outlaws chasing me.

All I could do was pray and say, "Oh goody, bad guys in front of me and bad guys in back of me. How can I miss?" Right then the story of Elijah and his servant came to me.

Seems the king of the country next to Elijah's home sent an army to kill him because of his good instructions to the army of Israel. The servant got up in the morning and saw the army of this evil king lining the hills around the town Elijah and this servant were in. The servant ran back in the house and told Elijah they were going to die, there was an army surrounding this little town. Elijah didn't even get flustered. He just asked God to show his servant His army. God opened the eyes of the servant so's he could see the army of God, which was huge and ferocious and more powerful than the king's army. Needless to say, the king's army got dealt with right smartly.

"Okay Lord. Let me see your army."

All I saw was the view between my horse's ears and I wasn't too happy with that. There was no army between Solomon's ears, at least not that I could see. Two ears and me didn't make for much of an army, either.

We took off to get in the tangle of trees and scrub before the ones behind us caught up any more. I couldn't believe my good fortune when there was no one waiting for us there. The tracks just kept on going. The dog tracks were still there on top of the horse tracks. A patch of cloth was on the ground partially buried by a hoof print. It looked to me like the dog's print had covered a big part of it.

What kind of dog was this?

I stopped just inside the dense stand of aspen and scrub, turned my Winchester toward the men behind me, and took another outlaw out of the saddle and out of the action. He fell next to the tree that had the slug in it that had been fired at me as I emerged from that opening earlier.

He went down and the two horses behind him rode right over the top of him. His scream wasn't pretty. I really do hate to see men die. God works in mysterious ways His wonders to perform.

I know it's Old Testament, but the Bible says that if you live by the sword, you will die by the sword. Somehow I was figuring that gun could be substituted for sword. But, then again, Jesus told his disciples that the time would come when they would need to sell their spare robe to buy a sword. Would gun fit there? I wasn't sure. It sure seemed like God was setting up a bunch of bad men to stand in front of my gun.

Would I die by the gun?

I quit thinking on the subject with that question.

Four shots were fired in my direction so I returned the favor with two rounds from the Winchester. Didn't hit anything important, but it made me feel better. It also scattered the crowd behind me.

Solomon decided it was time to get us out of there. I had to hold the horse back or we would run smack dab into the tail end man ahead of us. We rode slowly, moving from cover to cover always keeping an eye on the back trail. I felt like a dumb kid first time he saw the big city and all the big buildings with his head swiveling as fast as possible.

As we rounded a corner on the trail I saw a fork. One path went up the side of the hill and the other stayed down along the creek in a bottom that was widening. From where I was I could not tell which branch the outlaws had taken with Diane. Both trails led to areas of wide open country. The bottom was wider and had fallen into a different type of growth, small trees far apart. The uphill branch was hanging on the side of the mountain by a hair, a very fine hair.

I crossed the creek through a mess of brush and saplings to get a better look at the uphill branch. There were no tracks on it. There were no tracks on the trail along the stream, either. The revelation was a strange and unfathomable to me as the Revelation of Scripture must have been to the human writers. How could this be possible?

It was a cinch they had not turned around. We would have collided. There was no sign of brushing out tracks on either path. They must have gone down stream walking the horses in the water. I took the path along the creek and began serious watching of both banks for an exit point. The problem became that I had to check out every solid rock exit point very carefully which meant I had to ride up every shelf and rock bottomed side cut until I could be sure they had not used it for an exit and started off in a new direction.

I had done two shelves and three side cuts before I hit the right one. It was a shelf of sandstone three feet wide and angled off uphill and away from the stream. There was a beautiful campsite centered on a flat red rock that would have made a great dinner table and kitchen next to the fire pit. I could see where someone not too long ago had set their saddle and blankets on the ground not too far from the fire and spent the night. A reasonably new flour sack was draped over a limb to confirm my findings.

That shelf went on for a ways, but fortunately, I saw two fresh strike marks where an iron horse shoe had recently hit the soft sandstone. About two hundred feet into it and there was a silver disc and a shred of plaid shirt. Diane was still thinking. Not too far after that point the tracks became clear as the path hit damp clay and I could pick out individual horse's prints.

From the length of strides and position of the tracks I got to thinking they had started moving faster, but like a bunch of dummies they were going uphill and were going to tire their horses much faster. Having been on the trail for some time and on tired horses, they needed to find a campsite right soon or kill their horses.

The trail rounded a corner and started going down, at the bottom was a plume of smoke. Someone had just lit a fire of wood that wasn't very dry and I had a real good idea who it was. Sitting in the trail was the dog. The location was ideal if they hadn't started the smoke pouring into the sky. There was a ten acre hollow filled mostly with trees so close together you couldn't see very far into the patch of woods.

Looking around offered me no way out of the fix I was in now. Thinking on the crowd behind me and the location of the ones with the smudgy, I was the meat in the sandwich. 'Charge, always charge,' rang through my head. Solomon started walking down the hanging trail into the hollow as the dog stood and trotted into the woods. I lifted the rifle out of its scabbard and checked for a round in the chamber and a full magazine. That was about as ready as I could get.

Nobody challenged us in any way as we approached the thick woods in the hollow. The dog came out of the trees and moved toward the creek we had been following, disappearing around a pair of rocks. Still no challenge. Behind the rocks I found the dog laying down in a sunny patch of sand in the bottom of a dried up pool not six feet from a drop off into the stream thirty feet below.

So, now I was not the meat in the sandwich. I had a hidey hole just big enough for the three of us as long as only one of us stretched out at a time. It was defendable, but it would be a fight to the death, there was no exit except the entrance. I sat myself in the entrance behind a clump of brush I pulled out at the side and moved to block the entrance and waited.

Within moments, a man walked out of the woods not a hundred feet from me. I could have shot him with the greatest of ease except for the idea that it would blow my cover. There was no way I was gonna do any shooting until the followers caught up and joined up with the ones in the woods with Diane. Then and only then would I know how many and where they were.

Solomon nickered twenty minutes later. The horses in the woods responded and so did a horse coming over the hump into the hollow. Both sides thought the nicker came from the other group of friends. The following group of men saw the smoke in the hollow and pulled their rifles out in preparation of finding me. I had to chuckle at that idea. Unless there was a trail out the other side, and I hadn't seen one, I had them bottled up real nice. Of course I had no way of stopping a concerted charge of the whole bunch of them even if every shot was a killing shot. With ten rounds in the Winchester and six in the pistol, I'd be two bullets short of dealing with the crowd I figured was down there. Twelve men had just ridden in. From the sounds of things whooping and hollering down there, they must be old friends.

Two men walked to the edge of the woods and began walking back to the ridge on the trail. They were posting guards and the fox was already in the hen house. I guessed there wasn't a decent tracker in the bunch if they didn't see my tracks coming up that rise before the hollow.

Two hours later the dog woke me up with a paw on my lap. I looked around to see two more men coming from the woods walking up the trail with rifles in their hands. The changing of the guard was nothing fancy like I'd read about in a newspaper a couple years back, but that is what they did. I went back to sleep figuring the dog and horse were gonna be on lookout.

I was wrong.

22

I was awakened by a gun prodding my ear and a voice, "You listen here, boy. I will blow your head off if you move sudden like. Keep your hands where they are as Lefty gathers your armament."

I did.

"Now, stand up slowly, very slowly. One false move and you're meat."

I did.

"Walk on out here."

I did.

"Lefty, get the horse and keep him covered from behind."

He did. At least I suspected he did. I could hear Solomon walking not too far behind me as we walked out of the hidey hole and down to the tree line where we were met by three real bad men who welcomed me with a heavy handed slapping up-side of my head. I pretended to be knocked out and fell to the ground. They kicked me until I got up.

The voice with the gun said, "Stop. Boss man wants him alive and whole. If he screams loud enough the girl might sign the papers."

I just couldn't keep my mouth shut. "Not if I have any say in this, she won't."

"Then she's gonna die, Preacher."

Oh, so at least one of them had seen me in Denver or someplace earlier. "Lefty," the one that called me preacher was behind me, "Did you listen to my sermon?"

"Yeah. Didn't like you sayin' we's all sinners. I ain't never sinned in my life, yet."

"Did you just join this gang?"

"Nah. Did most of the horse wranglin' for the ranch until you come along."

"You must feel right proud riding with outlaws that are trying to take a ranch away from a woman after they killed her father, right proud." He hit me in the back of my head sending my hat flying.

"Just keep walking toward the fire."

It was more like stumbling toward the fire as I approached it. I saw Diane sitting on a log with her hands tied in her lap. She didn't look too badly abused. She was still wearing the plaid shirt even though the hem was looking a mite raggedy. The look on her face told me she just gave up all hope. I knew better. There was a hope that never lets a gal down. It wasn't me.

They tied me to a tree and gagged me. "We don't need no sermons so we just goin' ta make sure you cain't talk. You must think you are really bad chasing a group like us. Real bad."

I looked him in the eye and nodded as I tried to make my eyes smile. Once the tying was done they just walked away and left me there. Everson was nowhere in sight.

When they tied me I had set my hands in the position the magician showed me back in Kansas City. I worked my hands a bit. By working my wrists flat together, I was able to gain a lot of freedom. Whether I could get my hands loose or not was another thing. There was going to be a showdown here shortly. I was hoping.

I knew they weren't going to hang onto me for very long. As dangerous as they were I had beat them so far and they would want revenge and to make sure I wasn't ever on their trail again. Don't think I'm bragging here, it's just the truth. Given half a chance, this orphan sitting across the fire from me would be free and they would all be in whatever condition I left them in after I made the escape. I could end up dead amongst them, but she would be free.

It was as if she knew what I was thinking. She lifted her head and looked through the smoke at me with a pitiful smile on her face and shook her head. I nodded back. She just bawled all the harder. Her whole body convulsed from the sobs.

I had to do something before she had a total collapse.

The rag in my mouth was nasty tasting and caused me to try, without thinking about it, to shove it out and away from my mouth. As my jaw worked the bandana around my head began to slip downward. I was able to use my tongue to get the ball in my mouth moved above the head tie. I went into a shaking fit so I could dislodge it completely and drop it to the ground between my feet.

Something licked my hands.

The dog was here.

I froze wondering what to do now. I had a fighting partner in that dog. I looked over at Diane and nodded behind me. She looked at me, saw nothing, and went back to crying.

I laughed. I laughed out loud with the head tie on my chin. The whole bunch of supposed bad guys and outlaws jumped looking in every direction except at me. I said, "You big bad badmen all worried about a girl and a wanna be Christian preacher when nothing of this is going to benefit you one dollar's worth. That fat man you work for is going to get it all and see to it that none of you live to tell about this. You will have killed a woman. They hang men for killing women out here, don't they? Who wants to hang first? Or, do ya all wanna hang together?

"I have already killed and shot holes in a bunch of you. What? About half I'd say. You gotta kill me or there will be a witness to your killin' a woman. You gotta kill her cuz that's what the boss man wants and she can pick each of you out of a crowd when she gets back to civilization.

"Why do you let that fat man boss you around like he does? He says go get a girl and off you go. He says kill the girl and you'll do it. For what? Why? So the fat man can be rich while you work for $30 or $40 a month and food. Oh yeah, and you'll have to go steal the money he pays you with.

"Wait a minute. I have it. He wants a big ranch so he doesn't have to outlaw any more cuz you pitiful outlaws have done all the killing and robbing and hell raising on the roads and in the cities around here. You get blamed and he is rich. Well, you better kill us now and scatter before he comes in and kills you off one at a time after he orders you to kill us. Or, you could cut us loose and get out of here. I do not lie. I will never tell anyone who any of you are."

I quit. Then it hit me. They had listened and never tried to stop me. If I had been them with their evil minds, I would have just drawn my gun and ended all that speech. Instead, they had listened. They knew I was right. A few of them were looking at Diane shaking their heads. One was staring me in the eye.

"You know something, men. If you would get my Bible out of my saddlebags and cut my hands loose I could show you how to get forgiveness and change your life for eternity."

I pulled my hand loose from the knots and brought both hands around to the front. "Just hand me my Bible, boys."

It was like magic. Every one of them had a startled look on his face. Diane wilted into a pile across the log. Before my very eyes, this is true, the group of them faded into the trees and began saddling their horses and leaving. I reached down to untie my feet before the rope around my waist fell to the dirt.

They didn't leave us a thing to eat. One man walked back. "Ma'am, I am truly sorry for what I done. Please forgive me. I knew better."

Diane was fuzzy. She looked at the man, old, wrinkled, and tears running down his cheeks, and just nodded her head.

"You been forgiven, cowboy. Now go and sin no more. If you're looking for a job, see me in Denver in a week or two."

He turned and walked away. He said over his shoulder, "I just might do that. I wanna hear more about this forgiveness stuff. My

Ma usta talk of it when she drug me to the meetings. Shoulda listened, I reckon, shoulda listened."

We listened as he climbed to the top of the hump. Once the sounds of them retreating were gone I went to Diane, "It's over. We can go back to your ranch. How's that sound?"

"You worry me. How do you just talk 16 men out of killing us and then calmly tell one you'll get him a job and then tell me we'll go back to the ranch, my ranch, and get things back to where they were. I was scared to death. They were going to kill me, but before they did, they were going to. . ."

"Stop. It's over. There is nothing to fear except the usual things like snakes and such."

She just looked at me like I was some kind of a loco lunatic.

"Diane, I have a God that is in charge. I am not in charge." The dog walked up to me. "This dog came outta nowhere and has been in the middle of the whole thing. My horse belonged to the man who killed my Dad and that horse is a mind reader, or something of the sort. What just happened was me doing what that God I believe in told me to do. I don't ever want to kill another man. That God allowed me to end this with no more killing. Who knows, He may have a good use for a few of them, just like he has for me. Where you were seeing no hope, I knew there was hope one way or the other. It was all up to that God of mine."

I hugged the dog and asked him to watch things for a bit while I got some shut eye.

Diane said, "You leave a dog on watch?"

"Yup. He can hear and see better than I ever have or will. Who else better to be on watch? Where's your blanket?"

"I'll get it." She walked into the trees and returned, laid her blanket next to me and laid down on it. She pulled half over her. "Good night."

I swear she was snoring before I even found my horse, let alone my blanket. I have no idea how long it took me to snore, but it was day light when I quit. I awoke with the question on my mind of, 'what happened that the dog let them men sneak up on me in the hidey hole? Why didn't the dog wake me up then?'

I guess it was another God thing.

23

We were half a day down the trail to the Rafter B when it hit me. The fat man hadn't been there in the hollow. All those men were just hired hands, or at least working on shares. What happened to the fat man, Everson? How many men did he have still? Where were they? Was he still dead set on grabbing the Rafter B? There were a lot of questions and mighty few answers.

Long about mid-afternoon I saw a group of cows so I swerved off the trail to check them out. All were wearing the Rafter B except one old cow and a calf. The calf looked a might stringy and the old cow didn't have a bag to speak of. I shot the calf. Feeling bad about wasting a lot of meat, I rode off to catch Diane with only a hind quarter hanging on my saddle. We were going to have a meal tonight.

The sun was straight up the next day when we spotted the buildings of the Rafter B. "You wait here. I'll check it out and wave a bandana if it's safe." Having to use the bandana reminded me I was going to have to get a hat next store we found, my head was frying through the hair.

No one was home. I waived my bandana and Diane joined me.

Other than dirt, the place was a mess. Coffee spills, dirty dishes, a broken chair, back door leather strap hinge at the top was busted, and the beds had been slept in with boots and spurs on. New covers were needed on both beds. In the barn there were no oats left. The hay loft was a mess with cigarette residue all over the place. Did these clowns know nothing? Even I know better than to be in the barn, specially the loft, with a fire of any kind. The bunkhouse was a disaster. Food pieces all over the place and an obvious invasion of mice and rats destroyed the hominess of the place for me. I set up camp inside the barn next to Solomon.

Diane pointed out, "The two hands we left behind to watch the place are missing. My mother's ring and my jewelry, cheap stuff, are all gone. The gun rack is empty. All the spare rounds are gone. I did find my dad's hunting knife. It was stuck in the kitchen counter. From the looks of the counter, they left it there quite a few times. I will kill any of them I see. They killed my father and they have ruined this place, at least the memories. My mother's tintype is missing. She was a beautiful woman and I'll bet one of those cowboys is dreaming of her while he holds the picture up to the light. I'm sick, just plain sick of all this. Take me to Denver. I'll sell the place to the meanest bunch I can find and go to San Francisco."

"Let's give it some time for the dust to settle before you make any big decisions. I'm not ready to go back to Denver quite yet, so I can stay here with you and help ya put it all back together. Light a fire and let's eat."

"There's no food left except a few spuds in the root cellar. They broke all my canning jars, too."

"Not too bad for only being here a few days or so. I wonder what the inside of the home ranch looks like."

The sound of horses coming into the ranch yard called us to the window.

Two riders entered the ranch yard with hands on their pistol butts and reins. Both looked like it would only take a wrong move and someone would die.

I walked out on the porch after telling Diane to get the shotgun and stand in the doorway. "Howdy boys, what you looking so spooked for?"

"Two riders we met down the road a piece told us there was a couple openings for hands at the Rafter B ranch. This that ranch?"

"Yeah. Lite and set. We can talk."

The tall one had spoken first, but the short one, and he was short, said, "Them two sounded like there was a war going on over here. One was wounded and the other was just plain scared and never denied it."

Diane stepped out and asked, "What were their names?"

"Never did get their names, Ma'am. They just said they was making two openings and for me to see the boss." Shorty looked at me and said, "You be the boss of this outfit. I got the impression the bossman was an older man."

Diane stepped up and said, "I am the owner." She nodded toward me, "This is my foreman, boss, whatever you want to call him. He goes by Deacon."

The tall one said, "My name's Buck and this giant of a man is called Shorts. Don't let the size fool ya, he can whip his weight in wildcats any old day."

Shorts looked kinda embarrassed, "He brags on me so folks will pick on me and not him." He smiled, "Well, are there two jobs open here or not. If not we gotta get on down the trail."

I spoke up, "Can you work cows?"

"We know which end to drop a loop over if we can get close enough. Both of us have crossed the river and seen the boogers."

"You're hired. Toss your stuff in the bunk house and meet me here in five minutes. There is a shooting war going on here. Folks are trying to take the ranch from Miss Diane here."

Diane just looked at the two for a moment and then said, "I hope nothing happens to any of you cuz of me. I'm am going to make this ranch pay and its gonna be hard work for all of us, but now there are four of us."

Diane turned a corner to be talking rebuild and making a go of the place. She knew there should be money in the bank in Denver that she would have no problem getting when needed, and she knew the ranch had been making money. "So, why don't we make it make more money? Dad always wanted to add a couple of line cabins along the edge of the heavy woods, one to the south and one to the west."

"Excuse me, but wouldn't it be better to find out what's left of the herd and check out the graze before you start building projects for things that haven't been done because they weren't important enough. If there is no herd, there is no need for line cabins. If there is no herd, where did it go and how do we get it back?" the puncher named Shorts sounded like a wise man.

Standing not quite five feet tall in his high heeled riding boots, he still looked like a big man. Muscles rippled as he moved, his back was straight, the left side of his face had a deep purple bruise from a discussion with someone back down the trail and his clothes were well used up.

Buck was a good six feet tall, slim as a rail, and mad as a wet cat. "Them boys we met yesterday after meeting up with your old hands, was talkin' takin' the cows, Mizz Diane. They's talking about killing us till Shorts whipped their big man, not the fat one but the one that thought he could whip anything with skin. Shorts showed him the error of his ways. After that we just saddled up and rode out. Ten to two left us no choice and they never even tried to stop us. I think most of the cows is over to west of here. Leastwise, that's where we stashed the ones we found on the ride in here. Some of them critters need to be branded."

Diane looked at both of them before saying. "Thank you, you both have a job here as long as there is a here."

Ten hard days of riding showed us that most of the stock was still around. Diane figured she was a couple hundred short, but we hadn't worked much to the north yet.

At dinner that night, I said, "We need supplies. That sack of oats Shorts here found in the tool shed has helped us, but it's almost gone. Oatmeal mush and beef just ain't my idea of great grub. It might keep our ribs from showin', but it ain't making me any fatter.

A man's gotta have a gut if he's to be a big shot preacher, you know."

Diane said, "Hush up and say the grace."

Next morning Shorts and Diane rode for Boulder, she said it was closest, while Buck and I started digging the cows out of the brush north of the ranch house.

Five or six miles to the north we found over a dozen cows bellowin' without calves. All of them were bagged up to the leaking stage. "These here mama cows got calves somewhere. From the looks they ain't nursed in two days. Two days ain't much of a lead when it comes to trackin' them baby critters," Buck was angry. He pointed his horse north, writing big S's in the dirt with horse tracks as he searched for the trail of them calves. The cows kept up their chorus of bellows as I rode off to join him. My S's were made to the east of his, me knowing where the Lazy E was let me point right for it.

Half a mile later with the bellowing following us, Buck whooped and waived his hat. I waved back at him with the raggedy hat I found in the bunkhouse and rode over. Sure enough, calf tracks separated from the cow tracks. The cows had been forcibly pushed back by two riders while three moved the calves north. While we were sorting out the tracks, the cows trotted on by us still bellowing.

"Let's follow them," Buck shouted.

I nodded and we were off at a pretty fair clip to keep up with the cows. They didn't run far, maybe four miles at best, when we went over a rise and there below us in a patch of green grass with a trickle of water running through it, were a dozen calves. The cows called and the babies come a running.

One after another they hit a teat and commenced to sucking.

One after another they cried and backed off.

I looked at Buck, "That normal?"

"No." He shook out a loop and laid it over the head of the nearest calf. "Get down there and lay that poor critter down so's we can check it out."

I did.

As I was sitting on the calf I noticed a bit of milk running out of the calf's mouth. It was pink. "Buck, this calf is bleeding from the mouth."

Buck walked up and took a look. "Just what I thought. They done split the calf's tongue so he cain't suck. In a few days they'd be doggies and the mama's would quit trying to feed them. In a couple weeks them Lazy E cowboy rustlers will come out and round up the doggies, brand them with the Lazy E, and claim them forever with no way of tagging them as rustlers. Assuming of course that the Lazy E is doin' this."

"Let's drive them home."

"Let's leave them here and follow the tracks of the rustlers."

"Let's take a look at the horse tracks leading outta this place. I'll wager they go straight thataway." I pointed.

"Let's ride. I cain't stand a man that'd do something like this to poor little ole calf." He reached down and took the loop off the calf, climbed aboard, rolled his string, and we set out in the direction I had pointed. Sure enough the tracks led off that way. We followed until Buck said, "We cain't stand against the men in that crew. I make it 12 horses we been following. Let's go back and see what we can do."

We camped next to the calves that night and shoved them clear back to the barn the next day.

On the way back I asked, "How come them cows didn't follow the calves' scent back there at the place they was standing and bellowing?"

He went over to one of the cows in the corral that let him walk up close, dropped a loop, snubbed her off, and took a whiff of her nose. "Peppermint oil. They doused their noses with peppermint oil so's they couldn't smell them babies. When we took out after'em, they joined us knowing that riders are always around other cows. When we got close enough, the peppermint oil had worn down some and the scent came through. Off they went. Them full bags must be real painful." He hunkered down and started milking the cow he had snubbed off. She stood there and I'll swear she sighed.

We relieved them all, not much, just relief.

Sitting around the fire that night I looked at Buck, "Can you tell I'm not a hand?"

"Yeah, but you work. That's what matters."

I told him a bit of my history and Diane's pa getting killed. "I can learn, but most of all there's an orphan back at the ranch that needs help and that I can do."

"There are two more of us to help with that. We can shoot, but we ain't gun fighters. We'll stand with the brand and I like having you beside me."

24

Boulder was a five day journey there and back. I figured they would take ten at the least with Diane talking with the legal folks and the bank. I know she was going to talk with the Marshall and the situation with the Lazy E. She was also looking for two more hands to help with bringing back some breeding stock and horses. We waited and worked for two weeks and no sign of them. The oats were gone. We were eating our own beef and wild onions, with an occasional roasted prickly pear cactus pad.

Buck suggested we go look for them. I suggested he wait here until I got back. Buck had seemed like a good hand and wasn't going to back down without a good reason. We discussed options if the fat man came around and a few things Buck could do while I was gone. Didn't take me long to saddle up and hit the trail with two pounds of jerky in my saddlebags.

Just before sundown I met up with a herd. I rode in cautiously and met up with three rough looking hands. "Howdy. You boys driving them beeves anywhere in particular?"

"Yup." The big guy up front was real talkative.

"The brands are all different."

"I have bills of sale."

"You headed for the Rafter B?"

"Could be."

"Miss Diane send you to meet up with a man called Daniel?"

"Could be."

"I'm Daniel."

"I'm Will." He pointed to the man on his left, "This here's Tommy," and then he pointed right, "Cicero. Brought Tommy and me from Boulder, this here Cicero was lost out on the prairie looking for somethin' to eat he didn't have to pay for."

Cicero smiled with his mouth but not his eyes. "Man's gotta eat, don't he."

"Yeah, and I needed a cook. You ain't much of a hand with cows."

"I did the job didn't I?"

"Barely."

I ended the banter with, "Welcome. You got about 10 mile thataway."

"Figured." Will was very talkative even when he knew who he was talking to.

Then he said, "Gonna bed down for the night. Cicero makes a mean biscuit and some kinda thick gravy to go with the beans."

"Mind if I join ya for the night?"

"Glad to have you, boss."

"Boss?"

"Yup. Miss Diane said you was the boss and for us to take your orders or ride on."

"Where's Miss Diane?"

"Supposed to be behind us with a bunch a horses. Her and that Shorts fella."

"You don't sound like you like our Mr. Shorts." I smiled at that.

He grinned and shook his head, "First man to ever beat me arm wrestlin'. Smacked me down good, he did. I can work with him. Don't worry. That man is stronger than anyone I ever met."

"How far back you figure?"

"Two days at Boulder, or so Miss Diane told me. Should be almost caught up."

"I'll go check in the morning."

We bunked out after another hour of fireside chit chat. I took the sunrise turn at watching the cows who were a bit buggered by something off to the south. Come full light, three horses came trotting in, no saddles, no bridles, no lead ropes, just the horses. The way they took to the cows you'd thought they was cow ponies or something.

Tommy rode out to relieve me after a breakfast of coffee and biscuits with a few thin slices of beef - we had to finish the critter that had broken a leg a day earlier before it went rotten - mixed in. The coffee was great; first I'd had in a long spell of riding. The biscuits were a bit hard being leftovers from the night before, but were good for dunking. Tommy looked at the three horses as they wandered around the herd.

"I'd swear on my first month's pay one of them horses is one Miss Diane and Shorts were bringin'. I remember the socks and the blaze." Tommy looked a bit pale and worried as he said it. "I surely do hope I'm wrong."

Will was standing off by himself looking at the herd including the horses as another horse came down the slope to our camp. "Damn. I bought that horse myself," he yelled. "Something's bad wrong."

I saddled up as fast as I could. As I was mounting Cicero rode his horse over beside me, "Want a pardner? I can hit what I shoot at."

"Sure. Why not?"

Will was ready to go also, but I stopped him and sent him and Tommy on with the beef and the four horses that had joined up. "How many horses were they gonna bring?"

"Ten or more and their personals."

"I'll be back. Until then, do what Buck tells ya. He knows what needs to be done."

"I'll do it. You shoot straight."

"I usually do."

Cicero and I rode off following the tracks of the fourth horse.

25

We hadn't gone more than two miles when we saw the buzzards and crows circling up ahead. There must have been thirty of the carrion eaters circling, each go-round dropping lower and lower. We kept looking at each other as if to say, 'Oh, oh,' as we rode. Over the top of a rise was a dead horse. From the tracks and the blood trail it had been shot and made it this far before giving up. It hadn't been dead for long.

Kicking the horses into a faster gait, we spread out. I left Cicero on the tracks and I moved way off to the north where I could watch for the tracks of someone leaving the horse trail and heading for the Lazy E. I crossed no tracks, but Cicero found something. He was waving his hat when I turned that direction as I scanned the countryside.

I joined him.

Another dead horse. It was also shot and had traveled leaving a blood trail. It was the horse Shorts had ridden last I saw of him. Another horse had stood next to it as it finished dying and the tracks matched the first dead horse. Too bad that first dead horse had to die alone.

We rode, two men angry at the loss of horseflesh and concerned about how and where our friends were. We rode rapidly up the back trail, but with an eye out for anything, toward whatever there was to find. A dead stranger was the first find. This man had been shot through the body and didn't look pretty. A horse had stepped on his face. From the lack of blood, he had been dead when the stomping happened. We left him and continued. The trail turned sharply like there had been an ambush or something else serious enough to change direction so abruptly.

Tracks of many horses moving in all directions came next. Cicero was trying to make sense out of them when I spotted something that didn't look right down the slope. Cicero agreed it was something strange. We rode down with our guns out and ready.

We found Shorts. He had been dragged over the dirt and brush. The occasional cactus was an added pain for him. He was not a pretty sight. "Where you been?" he asked.

I looked at him again. "What happened to you?" He was propped up against a tree trunk, more blood than body.

"They thought they shot me, but they missed and hit my horse. He's over there somewhere." He swung his arm around half the horizon. "Then they drug me. I think some of these prickly pear thorns are in at least two inches. I've pulled out quite a few. They got Miss Diane. She was alive and running when I went down. She was alive when they paraded outta here heading toward the Lazy E. One of them said that this was the last time they were playing; from now on it was serious. I thought that was really funny, so I laughed. One of them threw a shot at me. Hit me here." He pointed to his right shin bone. "Broke it. There's been a horse wandering around down that slope in those trees. If one of ya would get him I could ride. My saddle is on a dead horse down that way just out sight behind the curve of the hill." Same sweeping arm.

I tossed him my canteen and said to Cicero, "You get the horse and I'll pick up the riggin'."

"Sure, boss."

I ran a coyote off the dead horse before I could get the rig. The horse was stiff. Two days at least this horse had been down. Two days Shorts had been leaning up against a tree trunk. Two days they had Miss Diane in their possession. I was getting mad. I was going to have to kill again and I didn't want to. I was going to have to take care of an orphan like the Bible says. The two ideas went together in my mind, but didn't come together in the Bible. Then I got to thinking of Samson who killed him a mess of Philistines with the jawbone of an ass just because they were messing with him. Then there was God Himself who ordered that all the evil nations in the Promised Land be killed down to the last child because of their evil ways.

I thought of folks in the New Testament that had died by God's hand for lying to Him, or the armies of Texas standing up to the evil of Antonio Lopéz De Santa Anna after the Alamo fight. Was God on the side of the Texans? It hurt just digesting all this in my head. I prayed.

With the prayer came the idea that God has always dealt with evil in different ways, but most times His person on the ground did the dealing, with God's power of course. There was no way Moses dealt with a couple million Hebrews for 40 years without God's power and wisdom. I felt strongly that God wanted me to rescue Diane no matter what it took as long as I gave them a chance to surrender.

Cicero and I got Shorts on the horse. I rigged some splints to hold that shin bone in place. One hunk of wood we smoothed and laid it along the bone to hold it straight. I slid a skinned Prickly Pear pad over the open wound before tying it and the splint to the front of his leg.

Couple of weeks and Shorts wouldn't have anything to complain about. We rode. I tried to get Shorts and Cicero to head for the Rafter B, but they would do nothing of the kind.

Shorts said, "You park me in a good spot, me and my Winchester will take care of anything that shows itself. I'm goin' with ya, or I quit and will go where I want."

"You wouldn't quit and you know it," I said as I swayed in the saddle, laughing.

"What's up with you?" Cicero shouted.

"Just thinking. Not too long ago I was saddle sore and aching. Now it seems like second nature."

"Gets that way right easy like when you're in the saddle all the time. I remember my first week in the saddle. It was not fun," Shorts added. "Ain't gonna be any fun now, either."

We rode along the tracks until the tracks of the herd wiped them out. It took us half an hour to find the tracks coming out the other side. We rode until the day was done, and even then we kept going until we just plain could not see. We camped on a stream that provided us with what we needed most, water and wood for a fire to brew some coffee. Shorts pulled the pot out of his bags and handed it down to Cicero who had the grounds in his bags. Not much in the way of a supper, but it would have to do.

Noon two days later we were looking down on the Lazy E again. No one was in sight. No smoke from the chimneys. No horses in the corral or tied out. We rode in with guns cocked and ready. Reckless? We were mad to the bone.

Shorts took one quick look around and started riding north. "Come on, they went this way. Looks like Wyoming is gonna be their new home."

We followed. No pieces of torn shirt. No silver discs. Just hoof prints from at least a dozen horses.

We followed.

We camped.

We followed.

We camped.

We caught up.

Cicero was out front and saw dust ahead of us leading into the trees at the edge of some rugged mountains ahead. If they got into those mountains we would be stuck with following on the trails that were available and could no longer pull off to camp or even work our way around them.

Shorts said, "I don't know this area a bit."

Cicero agreed.

That made three of us that had no idea of what was ahead. Cicero talked of a discussion he had in a saloon one time with a rider from

Wyoming. The rider said there were more dead ends in these mountains, if these were the mountains he had talked about, than there were good trails and even the deer get lost now and then. Shorts looked around like there was something lost before he said, "I did hear of a park in this area where the outlaws met to swap stock going north with those going south."

"Why would they do that," I asked.

"Easy reason. If you stole horses in the north, it'd be hard to sell them in the north. Same with cows. By making the swap, you end up with critters that no one's gonna know the brands they are wearing and you can forge bills of sale much easier."

"So, where is this park?"

"Beats me. I just heard of it, but this collection of mountains and such look like what that rider described to me. Said they weren't too happy to see strangers in the area either."

"Well, then. Let's announce our arrival and see what happens." I said as I pulled out my Winchester and headed for a small herd of elk a mile or more away. "Find a camp site and smoke it up. I'll be right back."

The young cow elk was easy to skin due to the winter fat she was working on. The three of us cut off some nice chunks of meat and began roasting them over the fire which was now almost smokeless except for the fat drippings sputtering as they hit the hot coals. The night closed in around us.

Morning brought company.

"Hello the fire," came out of the trees.

"Come on in. Hands in sight," Shorts hollered while Cicero and I found holes we had spotted the night before just in case. Just in case something like this happened, or worse.

The man came in riding a real fine horse that had not been ridden too far or for very long. He passed by my hole by not more than ten feet. "I got some biscuits in my bags. If you got the bacon, we got a meal." He looked around.

"Where's the other two?" he asked.

"What other two?" Shorts looked up. "I got coffee and nothing more. Even the coffee is puny, second pot with the same grounds. Lite and set."

The man swung down on the off side of his horse from me and Shorts, but right into the full sight of Cicero. Then I saw the rest of them coming in from behind Cicero.

I stepped out. "Tell your friends to keep their hands away from their guns or they will die."

"Who's gonna kill them?" he asked as he turned to see me.

The two other riders moved in close to Cicero and right on past him. If I hadn't known where he was, I could not have been able to see him. He was hidden that well. All them riders was looking around the fire and not expecting anybody that far out.

"Me." I turned out into plain sight for all to see. Pointing at the two riders, "Get off them horses and lead them in here."

"What's your problem?" asked the first man.

I let him think on it as the two men got off their horses. One of them made the horse move so his getting off would be hidden from me. His boot hit the ground and Cicero stuck his gun in the man's back, "Walk to the fire." He looked at the other rider who was some startled. Cicero was only five feet from him.

The first man was tall and lean. His clothes were well worn but neat. The gun on his left hip was worn, but ready. The tie down had been slipped off. He just stood there looking at me.

He said, "You're trespassing on private property."

"Didn't see no signs," Shorts said from his spot on the ground near the fire.

"You must have missed them. I am the owner of this ranch. I am Bordeau."

Cicero said, "Bordeau, ain't that some sissy wine folks back east drink?"

26

Bordeau drew his gun. As he brought it to bear on Cicero, I put a round in his gun hand taking his pinky off as the .44 slug slammed the Colt out of his hand.

He cussed shaking his hand flinging blood all over, spooking the horses they had ridden in on. "Mister Bordeau, I reckon we got off on a bad start. My name is Daniel. This is Cicero and the man with the bum leg is Shorts. Cicero is long on knowledge and Shorts is short on patience. I would recommend that you and your men come into the fire while Cicero takes your horses to the line. At the fire you can enjoy some of our weak coffee and pleasant conversation."

"I will kill you, whoever you are."

"Not with that gun or hand you aren't. Sit down and shut up." I was getting madder.

Cicero relieved the other two of their weapons, including a big knife from each, led the horses to the line, and returned to camp from a different direction, nodding to me as he leaned on a tree.

"Now then, Mr. Bordeau, we are looking for a young lady, our boss. She is being deprived of her freedom and her ranch by a fat man that owns the Lazy E ranch. I believe his name might be

Everson. Have you seen or heard of such a person or such persons who might also be trespassing on your ranch?"

He just stared at me.

I put a round between his toes. "Now, I took off your pinky and sent your gun to the scrap yard. I don't want you to doubt that I missed your toes on purpose. Did you see or hear of such people in the last few days?" I thumbed the hammer back for emphasis.

"No."

"He's lying, boss. I can tell by his eyes." Shorts swung his sixgun to point in Bordeau's direction. "Bet I can take an eye out without hurting him too bad. Might just smart for a while, but he'll never forget the day he met us."

"No." I walked to the other two men. One was a fidgety as a saloon gal in church. "You." I swung my gun to bare on one of the riders. "Have you seen or heard of any such folks around here lately?"

He flinched when the gun barrel just naturally pointed at his face. I lowered the aim to his fat belly.

"Well?"

He got to dancing like he had to find a tree.

Cicero stuck his gun in the man's ear. "Well?"

"Well?" Cicero pushed on the gun a bit and almost made the man lose his balance and fall over sideways.

The second man caught him and pushed him away. "Get away from me. Answer the question. You do know the answer, don't you? It's simple, yes or no."

Bordeau started to say something. I said, "You had your chance. Shut up."

"Everson was through here two days ago. Swapped out horses and headed north. I saw no woman or girl. He had three men with him, but swapped out 13 horses."

"Thank you," I said politely. "Cicero let him go. Give him back his gun and knife. He will need it to survive until he gets where he's going."

"Where am I going?"

"Anyplace you want, but I would suggest someplace far from here. I hear Texas is nice this time of year." I gave him my toughest look which I'm sure didn't come near to matching Bordeau's.

The third man said, "Can I ride with him. He and I been pards for two years now and only got in with this crowd cuz it looked easier than playing with cows and no one wanted us over the winter. I liked Texas and I ain't got no posters on me down there."

"Go. Cicero, give them both back their gear, shuck the shells from their guns and watch them carefully. I turned back to the leader of the trio. "Mr. Bordeau, whatever am I gonna do with you?"

"You better kill me or I will kill you soon's I can."

"That just is not the proper respect for your captor. Tell ya what, I'll leave ya here with your sixgun and all the ammo you want. You can walk back to the hole you crawled out of and know that if I see you again looking my way, you will die. Now go sit under that big fir over there and get some sleep." I walked to his horse and stroked the neck and mane. "I do like your horse. Maybe I'll just swap you for him."

"You ain't got anything I want." He was getting real grouchy.

"Your freedom?"

"You ain't gonna kill me, kid. You ain't got the guts."

"Let me see you again after today and you will find out the hard way. Without your pinky, you are gonna have to learn gun slinging all over again. And, I gather you are making your pay as hired gun."

He sat quiet.

"Who's your boss."

"I am the boss."

"No wonder them two wanted out. No man wants to work for a boss that can be beat by a kid. Them boys were looking for someone to take care of them." I stopped and looked around like I was thinking. "Get over under the fir; I'm sick of playing with you. Now get!"

He started to swing the right hand and I dropped him with my gun barrel planted across his skull. I grabbed his feet and drug him over to the spot under the fir. I sat him astraddle the trunk and tied both feet together, and then did the same with his hands. He was truly loving that tree. Bark was bristly. He wouldn't like that at all.

Shorts was roasting elk when I got done. Cicero walked back to the fire after seeing the two riders on their way. "Boss, what now?"

"We keep tracking. We are now sure that the trail is still the right one. They are headed for Wyoming. Whether they get there or not we don't know. We don't know a destination, we only know the direction." I looked to Shorts, "You up to this, partner?"

"Just try to leave me behind."

We finished what we wanted of the doe. I partially cut the ropes holding Bordeau, laid his gun next to him (didn't work anyhow), walked to Solomon and got him ready for the ride. We killed the fire and away we went. I decided it wasn't going to do us any good to try to sneak up on them and get the drop. So, we'd have to follow and take our chances on an ambush. We'd needed to make much better time and close the gap quicker.

The trail laid before us like the stairs to Heaven that Jacob saw. Only this time there were no angels on the trail. That was a truth for sure.

Due north we traveled. Finding a campsite an hour after we took to the trail with small boot prints around and all over the site gave us hope. No sign of blood or bloody bandages. There was one place where someone slept that was more than ten feet from all the others. I checked it out very carefully. Back up under a scrubby plant was the Rafter B brand scratched in the dirt and partially covered with a leaf. We were on the right trail for sure. Cicero said the fire was cold and he figured they were still two days ahead of us.

I said, "How'd you figure that?"

"That's what the man said when you questioned him."

"Well now, aren't you the smart one."

"Yes I am." He turned to climb aboard his horse, turned, "I'll bet they're headed for that pass and are probably moving up the trail to it right now."

"I am not going to argue with you. You're too smart for me."

Shorts yelled, "Let's ride. I can't take much more of you two clowns. I gotta find the circus you come outta and give you back." He was smiling.

I gave him a phony smile back and swung into the saddle. We made it to the bottom of the main climb by sundown. Like most trails to passes and saddles in this part of the world, there was a stream running not far from the trail. The sun was already behind the mountains to the west and the temperature was dropping. We built a fire well sheltered from the breeze and the trail, pulled out the last pieces of elk, and set to roasting. We ate it more hot than cooked so we could curl up in our blankets. Shorts took the first watch. He said his leg was hurting some and he wanted to get good and tired. I changed the dressing and saw there was no sign of infection or such. He was happy at that news.

Sleep came easy.

Cicero woke me up way too soon.

A hot bed of coals allowed me to stay warm as I listened to the last of the night.

Soon as I could see fifty feet, I woke up the other two, saddled the horses, and let them graze a bit before everybody was ready to mount up. Knowing the trail was gonna be steep and rocky, we checked the shoes on all twelve feet and found nothing to trouble us.

When the sun's rays caught up to us we were two miles up the trail and coming close to a false pass. The real pass showed behind the one we were approaching. "Cicero, you wanna check out that false pass and make sure there is no one waiting for us?"

Being in the lead he rode ahead and just as he got to within range of the pass he turned off the trail. He got off his horse and tied it in a spot anyone up top couldn't see. Then he went deeper into the trees to circle around their flanks if there was anyone up there. A good half hour later he was standing in the false pass waving us up.

I picked up his horse on the way.

Shorts was hurting pretty bad as we approached Cicero. I asked, "You gonna make it, friend?"

"Just try to leave me behind. I'll be riding when you quit."

Never underestimate the power of a man's pride on something like this. He sounded like he was trying to convince himself he could make it. I responded, "That convinces me," and meant it.

I handed Cicero the reins to his horse. He said, "There was a man here. He's behind the rocks over there." When he pointed I saw the knife cut on his arm. "That bad?"

"Nah. He just nicked me as he fell. I got him from behind and as he fell he spun. Dead on his feet, he got me with a touch."

I checked it out. It was a bit more than a touch, but should be nothing to worry about. Now I was riding with two men that were limited in their abilities due to the outlaws. I wasn't going to have much chance to do any talking to Everson or any of his gang.

That afternoon, late, we crossed the pass after I checked it out. No one was waiting to give us a well-earned reception. We rode through without feeling any disappointment concerning the reception not coming off.

The downhill side didn't offer any good campsites. We curled up on the trail. Cicero took the first watch and I got the last again. My eyes opened to a well-lit world. Shorts was leaning against a rock wrapped in his blanket snoring up a storm. Speaking of storms, black clouds were rolling over the mountain ridge to the west.

I yelled, "Let's get out of here. This is no place to be in a storm."

Shorts jumped to his feet before he thought. Fortunately, he didn't put full weight on that bad leg. "What?"

I pointed.

Cicero said, "That doesn't look good. I hate mountain storms. We have a ways to go to get below the tree line and under cover. You got a slicker, Deacon?"

"No. You?"

"No. Shorts, you got a slicker?" I asked.

"No. Our blankets will have to do."

The wind hit us hard enough that the horses staggered. We kicked them to go faster. Solomon wanted to run, but the shale and gravel wouldn't allow that. He'd end up with a broken leg and I'd have to shoot him if he ran. The first marbles of hail hit us as we ducked into the nearest clump of trees.

Cicero, in the lead, yelled, "Keep going. I can see a better place down a ways." He threw his blanket over his hat and most of his body.

Shorts and I did the same. It was hard to keep the blanket in place with the wind blowing as hard as it was, but without it the hail would be very painful. Solomon didn't like it at all and tried to get to Cicero in a hurry. I held him back.

The first crack of lightning hit the clump of trees we just left, as we entered Cicero's choice of hidey holes. The clump of trees burst into flames. If we had been there, we would have died.

"Thanks, Cicero," yelled Shorts.

I helped him off his horse and, with three blankets, set up a shelter that would keep most of the hail and the rain that followed off us and the horses. The horses were all spooked and hard to keep close under the shelter. Even Solomon in all his wisdom wanted to run with the wind. To do so would have been his death. The lightening might still take us away from this world. I had no fear of that, matter of fact, on some days it seemed like a good idea. God was in control, not me.

We waited. I tried to imagine what it would have been like if that lightning had hit us in camp just below the top. It wasn't a pretty picture at all. Fried cowboys and preacher did not sound too appetizing.

As I stood there trying to hold the blanket shelter together by sheer willpower, I got to thinking, which in the past has been sparse and not too productive. What had I gotten myself and Tor into? It had put Tor outta the picture. Yeah, I knew he could have walked away from my stupid ideas, but he wasn't that kind of man. How many times had Diane been with me and how many times had I let her get taken away? This prayer stuff was shaky at best. God wasn't my servant and He wasn't going to jump every time I said, 'Hey, God.' His plan was best, I knew that in my head and heart, but sometimes I questioned. Was that okay? Was I allowed to question God?

'What about the killing? Was that okay if I was protecting someone or even just me? Should I be doing what I am doing? Is this what God wants me to do or is this what I want to do because Diane is pretty and in trouble?'

I looked down at a sleeping Shorts, 'God, he is hurt. Let him get some peaceful rest and quick healing. (Now, was that telling God what to do or was it asking?) I am really asking, Lord. Your plan is best.'

27

Cicero was sitting under Solomon, who was calmer than the other two horses. He looked at me and said, "You praying?"

"Yeah."

"Pray for me, too."

"You a believer?"

"Once I thought I was, but then God allowed my wife and son to die in a cabin fire. I walked away from God and since then I've just tried to be a good man to their memory."

I had to think for a moment, "I think God will understand. Look at it this way, maybe, I ain't no expert. All of us are gonna die. Every single one of us. Why should your wife live forever? My Ma died. Was it God's fault or was it man's fault when he chose to not obey his Creator in the Garden of Eden? You really just didn't like the pain. I don't like the pain of not having a Ma to raise me up. If it weren't so wet I'd get my Bible out and read to you, but all I can do is tell you what I remember in my own words. God says if we ask in all seriousness, He will forgive any sin except ignoring Him. It says in there that we are sealed to Him by His Holy Spirit until He can make all the promises He has made come true in your life.

"Does that make sense, Cicero?" I looked him in the eye.

He shook his head, "How can God forgive me for the things I've said about Him when I was mad or drunk or just plain hurting?"

"I don't know, but He says He can and will. Try it if you mean it."

He looked at me and shook his head, but I watched his head bow and his lips start moving.

When he looked up again there was a peace shown on his face. "I think He said I was forgiven."

"What a load of hoowey that was Deacon. How could you believe that, Cicero? How?" came the weak voice of Shorts from the ground as he sat up.

"Don't ask me, but I did. You might wanna try it yourownself, Shorts." Now Cicero was the preacher.

Shorts got to his feet and turned his back on us, relieving himself into the rain, downwind of course. He turned back buttoning his fly. "If your God is so powerful and forgiving, can He heal me and forgive me the killing another man?"

I looked him in the eye and said, "Yes to both."

He worked his way back to the ground and turned his back on us.

Cicero gave me a look and I nodded my head.

We stayed quiet until the storm decided to quit and the moon broke through the clouds. The wool blankets were very wet as we rolled them and got the horses ready for travel. Cicero and I had to lift Shorts to his saddle and make sure he was balanced.

With the leg dangling to the stirrup, I checked his wound again. A scab was forming nicely. it was healing well as far as I could see.

Nothing looked or smelled bad. That was all I knew about wounds, other than the prickly pear pods for a poultice and Evelyn had taught me about that when I cut myself pretty bad one time.

We rode into a wet forest, the dripping boughs dumping water and getting us wetter than we already were. I looked for a place to build a fire in this wet swimming hole. Everything was soaked and so were we. Shorts didn't need the cold and chill as weak as he was and it wasn't doing Cicero and I any good either.

The trail was gone and so were the hoof prints. We'd have to worry about that the next day. A lightning strike off to the east lit up what looked like a shelter of some kind. Cicero saw it, too and turned off to check it out. In moments he was waving his hat and calling for us to come.

It was a recently abandoned cubby hole probably made by some Indian or trapper. There was a packrat's nest at the back, two feet deep and three feet wide, that had enough wood in it to warm us up a bit. Any heat was better than none. The boughs of needles over the top of the shelter were just beginning to drop from age so inside was fairly dry. Compared to the outside it was a dry desert.

Cicero got the fire going while I put up our two horses. When he was ready, we hauled Shorts into the shelter and I went back out to put his horse on the rope with ours. I watched them put their rumps to the wind and shift to three legged stances, which is a horse's way of saying good night. Thinking that was a good idea, I went inside to try for a nap myownself.

As I entered, Cicero tapped me on the shoulder and pointed to Shorts, who had tears running down his cheek. I said, "You okay, Shorts?"

He didn't answer for a minute or two as Cicero added wood to the fire in the middle of the shelter. "I just asked God to show me He's real by getting me warm and here we are."

"Don't expect that kinda service all the time," Cicero said.

"I agree. I've asked for all kinds of signs and the answers rarely, if ever, looked like what I asked for."

We were all asleep in a matter of minutes after we quit jawing. It's amazing how warm a wet wool blanket can be when the wet gets warmed up.

All the next day we rode ourselves in circles trying to find the tracks. We found a few horse tracks, but the group was never big enough.

Just before sundown we found the tracks. We had moved toward the north as we searched and figured we had covered a lot of country, but weren't sure how far we had gone. Whatever the distance was, these tracks were fresh. The dirt, or should I say mud, at the edge of the tracks was still curling into the deep tracks. We couldn't be more than an hour behind, if that.

How did they get so close? Had to be they found a spot to dry out and spent some time getting everything warm and dry, and all the people fed. I wasn't about to backtrack to find out. We were close and we were going to stay close.

Within minutes we found a camp site that served our purposes, lots of wood, a tree canopy to break up the smoke, and shelter from the night breeze. Just as it was getting dark, we built a high wall on the north side of the fire to keep prying eyes from seeing the fire and even then we kept it small. We had nothing to cook and nothing to brew. Water was the only thing on the menu.

Cicero broke the silence. "We gotta ketch them folks tomorrow if for no other reason than to get their grub. We sure's all get out cain't shoot something without telling them we're right behind 'em."

"You know, Cicero, that gives me an idea. Let's find us a spot in the morning for an ambush. Then we can shoot off one round like we was hunting and wait for a couple of them to come back and see what's goin' on."

Shorts' head came up, "I can sit and hold a Winchester without any problem. I can, I can. I'll be of some use that way, instead of being like a dead cow draggin' on the end of your rope."

"Shut up," I smiled when I said it. "If you was an anchor, I'd cut the line."

Cicero looked at him. "How you feeling?"

"Pain's tolerable. Bone aches. Toes wiggle. Butt is sore. Gut is empty. My attitude is one of wantin' to kill someone or blow up something. Other than all that, I'm fine."

We all got a chuckle out of that as we bobbed our heads. The jawing kept on for another hour as we worked to get the blankets reasonably dry. They weren't too wet what with the body heat and fire the night before.

My blanket felt better than it ever had before as I rolled up in it after telling Cicero to wake me at something that resembled one in the morning. He had taken a look at the Big Dipper and said, "Goodnight, Boss."

I awoke to see Shorts on watch and the night very dark. The Dipper showed it was close to 4 or so. I let him keep watchin' and rolled over to find a more comfortable position in the damp needles.

Cicero kicked me gentle like. "You gonna sleep all day, Boss?"

"I was trying to after I saw Shorts on the job."

Shorts smiled, "Just tryin' to be of some use. Let's go get'em."

"I'm all for that," was my reply.

We ate our water for breakfast and saddled up three tired horses. They complained a mite, but not enough to be aggravating. The sun was behind the mountain we were on as we worked our way to the tracks and, with Cicero out in the lead, we went after our prey.

My head or something was telling me that this was going to be a day, an eventful day. That's all I could latch on to. It wasn't as if it were going to be a bad day or a good day, just an eventful day. We rode into it with our minds and guns ready, like soldiers I would say.

Within minutes we saw their smoke and smelled the breakfast cooking. Oh, was that an bodacious smell. I drooled. Cicero shook his head. Shorts just kept riding.

Right soon we came up on a cut to the left that was lined with boulders at the entrance. Shorts stayed on the trail and Cicero and I went to check it out. It was as close to perfect for our task as any place I'd ever seen. The gunmen could come right through the boulders and into the cut where we could take them on up close and personal. Even if things went sour there were two escape routes for us to back out through.

"Hey, Boss, it just don't get much better than this."

"I agree. Let's get Shorts set up and then send out our invitation to the party out."

I rode down and got Shorts. Cicero got a smoky fire going for the outlaws to head toward and showed Shorts the place we thought the wounded man would work in best. It was right alongside the main escape route. There was a crazy looking rock that was slick but not too slick. Shorts was set in position on the rock with lots of protection and a simple slide to the ground next to his horse. All he had to do was shoot until it was time to leave, turn and slide down landing on his good leg, grab the reins, and swing up with as little weight as possible on his bad leg.

Cicero got set at the spot he had picked out for himself where he could use the same escape route that Shorts had. Me, I just parked my butt atop a rock dead in front of the trail coming in. The only bug in the ointment was the extra tracks coming and going on the trail, but that could easily have happened if we had really camped in the cut. All we could do was get ready.

I stood atop my rock and looked to Shorts. He nodded. Cicero stuck his arm in the air with a thumb up. There was nothing left to do except start the party. The hammer clicked twice as I pulled it back. I aimed up the cut and let fly with one .44 round, immediately jacking the lever and then inserting a round through the loading chute. The .44 on my hip with the blood red cross on the grips had six rounds in the cylinder ready for the fight to come.

I prayed. "Lord, I don't want to kill none of these men, but I think they aim to kill a woman, a defenseless woman. All of this is in

Your hands. It surely isn't in mine. Use me for Your will. Whatever, Lord."

We waited.

We waited some more.

Four men made an appearance like magic out of the trees near the trail into the trap. The lead man pulled up and pointed to the tracks in the dirt before swinging his arm along the trail, pointing at the rocks. Another man motioned them to get going along the trail.

We had planned that Shorts would take the man on the left, Cicero would do the man in the middle, and I would take care of the man on the right. We never figured on four. I had estimated two. Cicero said three. Shorts said he didn't care how many, he'd kill his share. We also agreed I would ask them to surrender before I fired. The two companions didn't care much for that, but agreed that if one of them made a move for a gun, we would open fire.

They came forward as if it were a Sunday afternoon ride to check out a water hole or something.

I waited until they had passed the three entrance boulders and stood up. They didn't see me concentrating on the trail like they were.

I yelled, "Surrender or die."

28

All four looked at me and grabbed for their guns. Three rounds hit them with the shots sounding like one. The survivor of that blast caught three slugs just as his gun was coming to bear on me.

Cicero slid off his boulder and eased into the death scene. One at a time he checked them for life. He looked up, "This one is still breathing." It was the one on the left. Shorts swore loud and clear. "He won't last long though. He's shot through both lungs from the looks of it."

Cicero bent over and kneeled next to the man putting his ear to the man's face. Moments later he arose. "He said he knew he should never have hung out with a man that would kill a woman."

He bent to check again. "He's dead."

'Four down and how many left?' ran through my mind.

We pulled the four to a spot where a boulder was in a position that the wind hollowed out a large hole under it. After stripping them of shirts, hats, guns and ammo, personal information, and money, we stashed them in the hole and stacked smaller rocks on top until they were well covered. Now we had four Winchesters, six Colts, and four fully equipped horses, all of which were top quality like most successful outlaws ride. Problem was, they had just gotten these back at the Bordeau ranch. Was Bordeau an outlaw? I might have to think on that awhile. All I knew was he wouldn't be using that gun hand of his for a long time.

We backtracked the quartet to their campsite, which was abandoned. The fire had been drowned and steam was still rising.

I looked at Shorts, "You figure they heard all that shooting and took off?"

"Nah," he replied, "They were probably leaving anyhow, figured his boys got the men following them and they'd catch up. Why'd we take the shirts and hats off them?"

"Well, let me tell you what we are going to do next," and I did.

After washing the shirts in the stream near their campsite, we headed after the Lazy E crew with the shirts flapping in the breeze from over the saddles of the extra horses. The hats were tied to our own saddles.

Long about noon we spotted our targets riding over a hill ahead of us. We were still in the trees so they didn't see us. One man stopped at the top and dismounted. Cicero said, "Lookout. One man to watch the back trail for a spell."

Shorts nodded and I reached for a shirt.

Within a short period of time we were the three survivors of the shootout riding to catch up. We were dressed in the shirts, wearing the hats, and riding the horses of the foursome that came to kill us.

Sure enough, as we got close to the lookout, he waved, climbed on his horse, and rode off to the join the others. We just kept our gallop steady and soon we were standing on the top of the hill looking at one man riding after seven more out on the flats. The lookout rode in amongst the others and they just kept on going.

One or two looked back.

We waved our hats.

Resting the horses allowed the outlaws to move on down the trail and into a countryside that was broken and would only allow them to see us for a while longer. Once they lost us we could catch up or even get into them before they realized the trick we had pulled.

The ride became one of close the gap, but don't catch up. They weren't lollygagging on the trail. We weren't either.

As we entered the broken countryside, we got a lot more cautious. It was a place that lent itself to ambushes and other nasty tricks. There was also the possibility that one or two might hold back just to find out what happened. I was almost hoping for that. We were still riding armed for bear and even had spares. I had the butt of my Winchester on my thigh and a second one in the scabbard. There was a Colt hanging by a piggin' string from the horn of my saddle and another tucked in my belt. Both were .44's of the same model as my .44.

All I could think of was, 'Bring on the bears.'

Two men did drop back to visit with us and see what happened. Unfortunately they died as their guns cleared leather. The real unfortunate side of that was now we had six riders ahead of us. Five of which were outlaws and one was Diane, we hoped. The problem became one of possible ambush and another of hostage.

Just as we were moving forward again, we heard horses coming our way. I fired a couple of shots just to make them think the fight was still going on and they would be able to help their side get rid of the terror behind them, us. It worked. They rode right into us with guns drawn and fell off their horses with guns in hand. One fired just as he hit the ground and took a chunk out of Cicero's left arm a hand span below the shoulder. It was on the underside of the arm and was bleeding in squirts.

I ripped my bandana out of my pocket, wrapped the arm, and tied it as tight as I could get it. The bandana slowly turned red, but a second wrap with my own shirt seemed to do the trick. Shorts moved slowly forward with a sixgun in each hand, his Winchester hanging by a string from the horn.

Cicero said, "I'm okay. Let's get this finished before the pain really sets in."

There were now four ahead of us. Three outlaws and one young lady, we hoped.

We rode slowly, with Shorts out in front and Cicero in the rear. I kept the Winchester on my thigh, but it was in my left hand with the reins. In my right hand was a Colt, six rounds loaded. I signaled a stop with an air blast between my teeth. Shorts pulled up. Cicero and I joined him.

"We're going to get ambushed if we stay on this trail. Look how easy it was for us to deal with the last four men. That's how easy it would be to deal with us at this point. Got any suggestions?"

"Yeah," said Shorts. "You try to circle them by riding high above all this badland stuff and we follow the trail. If you can draw their attention, do that and we'll hit them from another direction. If you can't, you ambush them and we hit them from behind. If you see they have an ambush for us, let us know even if you have to start the shooting."

"Sounds solid to me. Do either of you know anything about this trail or country?"

Cicero answered, "Yeah. North of here somewhere is Wyoming. Not too many more miles and the country widens out and there's a long, wide open plain at about 8,000 feet or so, but I have no idea how far and in what direction. Went through there from Fort Collins to the Great Salt Lake just to see what it looked like right after I got into this country. Wasn't too impressed with the lake. Cain't do nothin' with salt water except smell it."

"But, you don't know nothin' about this country? Right?"

"Yup."

"That is a lot of help. Next time keep it to yourself, Cicero. I hurt too much to be listening to travel stories with no sense to it." Shorts wasn't happy.

"Grouch."

"Yup. Wait till that little nick you got starts to heal and see how it feels."

"Boys, we got a woman to rescue. Let's ride." I looked around to see the dog walk out from behind a clump of rock on the higher ground and start to trot up high on the side hills. Looked like a good route to where I could look down on the badlands where everybody else was gonna be for a while.

"Luck," said Cicero.

"Skill," said I.

"Cow plops," said Shorts.

"Grouch," said Cicero and I as I lost sight of them.

I was riding one horse and dragging another as I followed the dog. Thing that amazed me was that none of those men had any food in their saddle bags. What were the folks we were hunting eating? Didn't make any sense to worry about it. Hopefully, we would be eating with Diane by dark.

That was a pipedream, only I didn't know it then.

The dog led me higher and higher, riding right out in the open. I could see both parties on occasion, but never together. The two on my side of the argument were moving slow and easy like along the trail. Every time I saw them I waved. If they waved back, I pointed to the other crew so they knew where they were and that they were all together.

An hour later the dog whined at me while he looked down on two of the gunmen stopping at the junction of a side cut like the one we had used in the badlands to set up an ambush. I couldn't see where the fat man and Diane - I was sure it was her - went. There was no sight of the two on my side. I waited with the ambushers in my sights from a long way away. The dog just sat watching. I figured that if they raised a gun, I'd shoot. I might hit one of them, but I would surely warn Cicero and Shorts.

One of them raised his Winchester and put the butt to his shoulder. I fired.

The shot splattered off a rock six feet from the outlaw I wanted to hit. He ducked. Shorts rode into the ambush with guns blasting until he went down right after I fired my second shot. The rifleman went down hard at the same time. He had been squatting and unfolded enough to hit the ground hard enough to bounce. He was out of the picture.

Shorts's head whipped back from the rifleman's last shot. He hit the dirt landing on his bad side and didn't move. Cicero rode in

The second outlaw tried to get on his horse and leave, but chose to stand and fight it out with Cicero. He fired. Cicero spun around and off his horse, landing on his one good hand and both feet in a crouch. His sixgun spoke from ground level and I watched the second outlaw fold. Cicero fired another round that caught the bad man with his gun coming down for another shot and spun the man around. The outlaw squeezed the trigger as he died and his last round caught Cicero somewhere in the body.

Cicero tumbled and laid still.

I rode down to check on my friends. As I rode I prayed, 'Don't let them die, please.'

The gunmen were never going to shoot another round or see another sunset. I almost wilted at that thought. All this killing and dying just wasn't my thing. I could do it, but I surely did not want to.

Shorts was dead when I got to him. The round had caught him on the tip of his nose and went all the way through, leaving a mess on the back of his head. I covered his face with the hat he had been wearing.

Cicero was shot, but alive. One bullet had caught him in the ribs right under the wound on his arm. The second round caught him in the other arm, breaking a bone just above his wrist. Two wings clipped and a furrow along his ribs put him out of action.

Catching up the horses I realized the dog was nowhere in sight. Every time he shows up, it helps the situation, so where does he go in between? Is he off in the woods watching? Is he tracking the bad guy for us? What and where, big questions.

Checking the saddlebags, I found a can of beans and a pouch full of corn meal. Oh, yeah, there were guns all over the place and horseflesh aplenty, but right now I drooled over beans and corn meal mush. I had to use three shirts to get Cicero to quit leaking before I could get him set up so I could go after Diane alone. He would have no problem getting on his way, but he was going to hurt for a long time.

A quick fire, heated beans, and a slurry of corn meal mush filled our bellies. I left the rest of the corn meal with Cicero and set him leaning against a soft rock with guns at hand and three blankets. All the horses except Solomon were his to keep, also.

"I hate to leave a man down, but I gotta go."

"I understand. I'd do the same in your shoes. I'll meet ya at the ranch if ya don't catch up with me after you get the girl."

29

"If you leave this place, go back along the same trail we came on. I'll catch you." I was hoping out loud.

"Yeah, that sounds good. I'll pull out in the morning after I eat this fancy meal you left me."

"I can take it if it doesn't measure up to your standards."

"Anything's better than nothing."

"Adios." I pulled Solomon onto the tracks of two horses heading up the side canyon.

I lost their tracks a dozen times in the rocky ground, but each time I just kept going the same direction and there would be tracks not too far up the trail. I was tired and hungry by noon and decided to take a break at the next spot that suited me. I could have used that dog right about then.

A shady spot near a small rivulet of water beckoned me and I took advantage of the invite. As I ducked my head to swing down from Solomon's back, the whip of a slug went past and the sound of a rifle shot came rattling through the trees. My hat went flying and Solomon lunged, dumping me in the dirt. Solomon took three more steps and stopped.

I rolled behind a downed tree and tried to figure out where the shot came from. My hat lay in the dirt not ten feet from me. I could see a hole in the brim on the back side. The shooter must have been behind me. A back shooter is no one to mess with. A real man will meet you and make his challenge face to face, but scummy cowards shoot people in the back.

The dog stood not twenty feet from me, sheltered by a rock and a tree.

"Thanks for the warning," I said looking him in the eye.

He trotted off into the woods.

"Bye."

Then it dawned on me. I followed the dog. After a hike up the hill he stopped looking off in the direction I had been traveling. Two riders were just topping a distant hill and going out of sight. "You could have told me to bring my horse."

The dog trotted after them. I went back for Solomon.

By the time I returned to the spot where the dog and I had separated, it was dark enough to know I was not going to do anymore tracking today. I took a nap.

The moon climbed high enough to do some good long about midnight. Half a moon stood out amongst a beautiful sky of stars and I could see my tracks coming in to this spot. Solomon walked over to me as if to say it was time to git. I threw the rig on him and we did.

Tracks leaped out of the dirt as we topped the hill where the two riders were last seen. I put the moon off on the far side of the tracks to help build a shadow in the tracks making them easier to follow.

Over the next three hours I was off and on Solomon as the tracks moved through different terrain. Once in a large spread of sage where all was in deep shadow, I had to get off and walk along bent over in order to see the tracks. Another time I had almost gone to sleep, awakening suddenly I found that Solomon was plodding along the tracks of our quarry. I wrapped the reins around the horn and let him go. He stopped at a point the tracks led to hard rock and there were none to see. I got off and kept going in the same direction. After a dozen feet or more there was a scratch, another a little further, and finally they were back in dirt.

Just as the sun was beginning to put a bit of light in the east, I saw their fire pit full of glowing coals. We stopped and the dog walked into sight right in front of me and parked himself as if to say, 'What took ya so long?'

I looked over the dog to the campsite. Someone threw a hunk of wood on the coals making the sparks fly. Not a lot of them, but enough to let me know someone was awake down there. Leaving Solomon there, I headed down the slight drop to the camp on hands and knees.

The camp was larger than I would imagine they would need. A man squatted at the fire coaxing the heat out of the coals to catch the wood he had put on top. A coffee pot sat on the ground beside him. I could see another person wrapped in a blanket on the far side of the fire

Diane!

I slid my gun out and moved toward the man at the fire. Twenty feet away I said, "Put your hands in the air and stand up slowly."

The man froze in his position at the fire. Slowly he began to stand. I said, "Diane, it's me, Daniel, get out of that blanket and come over here to me."

The blanket exploded.

The dog landed in the middle of the blanket.

A gun went off from under the blanket.

The blanket froze in place as the dog stood atop the rounded form.

"Get this animal off of me. Who you calling Diane anyhow?"

I looked real good at the man who was now standing with his hands up. He was well built, but not the fat man. What was going on here?

The dog backed down and a man emerged from the blanket. He, too, was slim and not the fat man or Diane. My jaw dropped.

"Who are you, Mister Daniel?"

I stood there silent, gun in hand, hammer back, and could say nothing.

The man at the fire asked, "You lookin' for a heavy man travelling with his daughter?"

"No. I'm lookin' for a fat man with a hostage named Diane."

The man on the ground asked, "Was she ugly as a twenty year old post?"

"No. She was pretty and well built."

"That must be the two that ate with us last night and then kept riding even though it was dark already."

I let the gun barrel drop and set the hammer down. "Sorry fellas, I was trailing them and you looked like them in this mornin' light."

"You saying I'm fat?" the man at the fire asked.

The other man laughed. "Mister Daniel, I'm glad you didn't come in shooting. We'da both been dead and you would have killed two somewhat innocent men; us."

I still couldn't talk. The dog looked at the two men and walked into the woods.

"What's with the dog?"

I finally found my voice, "He shows up from time to time. I don't know if nor when, nor where he come from, but he sure is handy sometimes. Don't understand him not knowing you two weren't who we was looking for."

"Now that you're here, want some coffee."

"I'd be forever thankful. Sorry for the wake up."

"It was kinda sudden, but the chill in my spine might just make me travel further today."

The man from the blankets asked, "Tell us about them two. If she was a hostage, he had her under control. She never let on."

"She didn't want to die after watching you two die," I said.

I spent the next hour sharing their coffee, bacon, and beans, while I told them my story. They never interrupted; they just kept my cup full. At the end I said, "I gotta get goin' and get Diane back to her ranch safe and sound. Much obliged for the feed. I ain't had a real meal since I don't know when." My stomach was somewhat prominent when I stood up.

"Talk about a fat man," the cook chuckled.

THE DEACON

The other man rolled his blanket as he asked, "You really were a phony preacher until you got to believin' your own preaching. Don't that just beat all? Where ya gonna preach next?"

"Denver, I hope. If I get through all this in one piece. Sounds like that fat man is right cagy. He just keeps giving me the slip. Again, I am sorry for the sudden wake up call."

"See ya in Denver, Preacher."

"I prefer, Deacon. I'm God's servant and deacons are servants. I guess preachers are, too, but I don't have the right to call myself one."

"The Deacon. That's quite a handle for a young fella like you. Have a safe journey to Denver by way of the fat man. I wanna hear ya preach. Maybe even I'll believe."

I climbed on my horse, looked back, "You boys ever get in the area of the Rafter B, stop in," and rode off in the direction the two pointed and the tracks in the dirt led. Where those tracks would end, I knew would be an ending to this episode in my life.

Within an hour I found where they had camped. The coals were still warm. I checked the tracks as well as I could. It looked to me like Diane was doing all the work while the fat man watched from a cozy flat rock near the fire.

An hour later I noticed the tracks were getting further apart and more dirt was kicked up by each hoof. I was thinking on that when it come to me that they had started moving faster. Had they seen me? Was there something else that would cause them to run? There weren't any bear tracks or other wild critters that might have scared them. Even if it had been a critter, the fat man had guns and could have taken care of that issue.

They must have seen me.

I looked at the back trail. I had topped a rise and then dipped and topped out again. They could have seen me on the first top and been gone by the second. I had been seen.

That changed everything. I didn't know the country. There were no towns around that I even had a hint of. There had not been a ranch or signs of one in days. All I could do was keep on following and pray that I would see them first next time. If I didn't, it was a sure bet that I would die at the hand of the fat man.

I prayed and rode on along the tracks.

The dog appeared ahead of me with his nose down and very obviously tracking a scent.

"Well, thank you, Lord." A smile grew on my face as I watched the dog stay just far enough away that I would be a long shot for a pistol if he tripped over the fat man. I shucked my Winchester and set its butt on my thigh, hammer back and magazine full.

A mile or so farther the dog jumped off the trail and I hit the dirt. Solomon stood over me like I was some crazy new-fangled rider. A shot broke the stillness. It didn't come my way, but I could hear it whack into a tree trunk near where the dog disappeared. I moved through the trees and that horse followed me. He had never done that before with bullets flying. I wondered why he would do it now. I passed a large pine of some kind and he stopped behind it. Now I knew.

I heard another shot. This time it rattled a couple of limbs above my head before smacking into a tree somewhere behind me. I was getting shot at. Peeking around the tree on the far side of where I was last, a puff of powder smoke lifted ever so wispy from a copse of young firs about 50 yards in front of me.

The girl screamed.

I'd had enough. I ran twisting and turning one way and then the other, dodging around trees and over logs until I was not too far from where the shots were fired. A nice soft bed of pine needles up against a fallen log became my home for a few breaths as I tried to get enough air. Another shot smacked into my log, but it didn't come through. I waited.

Another scream.

I crawled to the end of the log where there was a large root ball and a hole. I entered the hole and found myself sharing it with a rattler, a black tailed timber rattler to be specific. He, maybe it was she, wasn't happy.

I moved on in a hurry. My hurry caught the fat man flat footed. He didn't get off a shot before I ducked into a small wash. The sand was damp, but there was no water running. I peeked. Nothing. I started to peek again when sand flew over me and a shot sounded. I ran to a large tree and stood behind it for dozen breaths before taking a look

I was now about 20 yards from the fat man's firing spot.

One more scream.

I ran straight at the spot watching for the barrel of a gun to show. A slug whipped by my head. A puff of powder smoke rose. I was still charging.

I fired and jacked the lever. I fired and fired and fired, until the hammer went click. The Winchester hit the dirt as I cleared the first bushes in front of the spot. A slap on the rock next to me was followed by a singing slug flying away and a puff of smoke not 15 feet in front of me.

My sixgun came out and three rounds went into the spot just under the smoke before I leaped through the crack between two fair sized boulders landing in the middle of the fat man.

He was bleeding from the corner of his mouth as he breathed a gurgle or two. His eyes came open as he gurgled one more time. He grimaced. He died.

"Diane, where are you?"

30

"Here." She called from a few feet away, sitting on the ground behind the bigger of the two boulders. Her hands and feet were tied.

I fell to my knees in front of her, untied the loose knots, and helped her up. She threw her arms around me and kissed me. "Thank you. You saved my life again. He was going to kill me. That man told me I had one more sunset to see and then he would kill me if I didn't sign the papers for the Rafter B. I kept telling him you were going to kill him and he would have nothing. Oh, Daniel, you saved my life."

She fainted.

I whistled for Solomon and looked for the horses. Solomon trotted in. Diane and fat man had to have some horses around here close so I went looking.

An hour later we set off for the home ranch, back trailing all the way.

Diane told me about the fat man as we rode. He was the owner of the Lazy E, Toby Everson. He wanted the Rafter B because there was gold in the hills on the south side of the ranch, the deeded side. Diane's father and mother had homesteaded a section each in those rolling plains and her father had paid every one of his hands to homestead a chunk and then sell to him. He paid them well for the land and for their job on the ranch, $5 above the going rate for hands in the area.

Diane knew nothing of the gold until one of the Lazy E hands let it slip while they were running from us.

I asked why they ran.

"Oh, Everson wanted the ranch right proper. He wanted me to sell it to him. I told him it would be a cold day down south before that would happen, and then you came along. Something about you scared him stupid. He started running and you kept on following. Every man he sent was lost, they never came back. You were a jinx to his plan. Two of his men, two in the first ambush, were professional gunfighters - Bordeau or something like that and a side kick named Twisted - and he had hired them on their credentials of being in a couple of grazing wars. What is it about you?"

"I don't know. I just set out to get you back to your ranch like your father asked me to do."

We never caught up with Cicero. We'd see his tracks from time to time until on the third day the tracks were even gone. I circled a bit looking for them, but found nothing. If he made it this far, he'd make it all the way to the ranch.

We arrived at the Rafter B the next day. The wind was blowing causing brush to roll across the yard and no one was home. After I cared for the horses we had brought in, Diane called me to eat. She was at the table when I arrived. I ate like there was no tomorrow, at least until I was so full I was sick.

I darted out the back door and unloaded on the dirt. She wasn't far behind. We sat on the half log seat and laughed. "You got more where that came from?" I asked.

After eating like a normal ranch hand, I sat and thought about all that had gone on. For some reason I was troubled.

I could tell Diane was feeling the horrors of the past episodes. Her father was dead. Then there was the kidnappings, the rescues, the rides, the lack of hope, the death all around her, the lack of sleep, and all of it was affecting her as I watched. She fumbled through the cupboards looking for a pan and then needed a sharp knife. There were three on the end of the counter just out of sight, but she went through everything before she stumbled on to the three knives. She seemed really pleased with herself when she found them.

I decided I didn't need any more food and told Diane I was going to bed down in the bunk house.

Along about somewhere in the night when it was dark, shouts started in the yard. A gun was fired. A scream came from the house. I went out the door with a gun in my hand and my body covered with not much except the blanket. It was a good thing I recognized the bean pole frame of Buck standing in the moon light, gun drawn.

I yelled, "Don't shoot, Buck," and put my gun under my arm with the barrel pointing backwards.

Buck said, "Who the heck are you?"

"Daniel. Diane is in the house."

At that time Diane come to the door with her robe covering her night clothes. She must have lost some weight, the robe hung like she must have been a bit heavier, not fat of course, it was just out of proportion somehow.

I called to her, "Diane, it's just your cow hands coming in. Go back to bed. We'll get organized in the morning."

"What was all the shooting about?"

"Coyote in the yard," Buck said.

"That mighta been my dog," I said.

"I missed him. It was like he disappeared," Buck was shaking his head.

Motioning Buck and Tommy inside and turning back caused me to drop my gun which made me bend over and using the wrong hand to pick it up caused my blanket to fall away and leave me bending over naked. I blushed all over.

"Even in the dark, I can see the shine, Boss," Tommy yelled.

Diane laughed and went back in her house.

I spent an hour or so jawing, catching Tommy and Buck up on all the latest with Diane. Buck ended it with, "We ain't finding many cows on this place with the Rafter B brand. The new stock is settling in well. We've moved a bunch of Lazy E and a few of a couple of other brands off to the north over the big ridge. We're working the south side now and not much is showing. Saw some funny stuff off yonder," he pointed, "Like someone's working the ground and a hole in the canyon wall."

"I'll take a look at that tomorrow. Heard something about others working part of the ranch. We'll see. Goodnight all." I fell back and pulled the blanket all the way up.

The food bell clanged and my eyes opened to bright sunlight coming through the one window in the bunkhouse. Every other bunk was empty. I emptied the one I used and grabbed for some clothes to cover my nakedness and ended the dressing by pulling on my boots. The table in the kitchen was set for four. A plate from the counter, a spoon from the pot, and within moments my plate was full. Wasn't sure what it was, but it smelled like good food.

Diane came from her room with the same clothes she had been riding in, nothing was different.

"Why no clean clothes?"

"I need to wash up first."

I looked around. "Buck, fill that bucket will ya and let's get it on the stove to heat for a bath for the lady."

I finished my meal and trotted outside to a #2 wash tub I had seen hanging on the back of the house. It came off the nail easily. In the bedroom it went. I lit the lamp for warmth. Then a blanket was up to cover the window completely. The bucket of hot water was brought in and dumped in the tub, a couple buckets of cold water were hauled in, and Tommy came up with a bar of stinky women's soap from the kitchen under the sink. "Now, your bath is ready, Miss Diane, enjoy."

Buck tossed her a towel from the stack on the top shelf of a closet between the bedrooms, "Found these a couple days ago when I figured the water in the horse trough was warm enough for my ever' three month's bath."

"Why thank you, boys. I'll be awhile getting all this squished in dirt outta my pores. May even need another bucket of hot water."

Tommy said, "I'll get the bucket full and heating. When you need it I'll bring it to ya." Just as he finished he realized what he had said and turned as red as a ripe apple. "I mean, uh, you know, uh, awe forget it. I'll put the bucket on the stove and you can do what ya want with it." He got up and walked out with the empty bucket.

Once the rest of us regained our senses, off we went to get our chores done and move south.

An hour later she was still bathing.

I yelled through the door, "We're leaving now. Off to the south."

It was quiet for a moment, and then. "Be safe. I do not want to bury anyone else."

"I agree."

31

Our saddle bags were full of food and ammunition. Each of us had a few things we thought were important. I had found a pointy tipped hammer in the barn that I figured might come in handy and stuck it in my bags along with an old shirt of someone's I had found in the bunkhouse. Actually, I had found two. One I was wearing and one was stashed.

It was a good half hour before we saw our first beef, a cow with a calf about two days old. The brand on the side was Rafter B. An hour later we found a bunch of six cows with four calves. "Calf crop ain't too bad," Tommy said.

Buck had his opinion, "This ain't much of a beef outfit. We shoulda found a couple hunnert by now the way we been zigzagging all over the countryside. This is just what we did yesterday, Boss, only it was a couple miles thataway. Someone has either been lying to himself in his tally book or this place has been stripped. I think it's been stripped. That corral we found the first day out had been used. Cows in there for a couple days. Then the tracks go east. East is where a market might be. Them mines over around Golden and such make for a great place to sell a head here and a head there. Man could make more money with beef than with a pick in that country, unless he hit the mother lode, of course."

"What about this side? How do you figure this?" I said.

"Well, boss, I agree with Buck. Now for this side, there just ain't no tracks. Except for the few head we done found, there just ain't no other tracks. I'm thinking they started on this side. Only way to find out is go over to the east and see if we can come up with a serious mess of a herd going yonder."

"Sounds like we got a beef problem for the little lady. What about the dirt shifting and digging? How far away is that?"

"Over thataway a mile or so, but we'd have to go back a couple miles to get a route in there. That's some pretty rough country that happens of a sudden. If you don't go at it just right you'll miss or get blocked."

"Let's ride." I kicked one of the new horses into a lope. Solomon had the day off.

We entered the craziest valley I ever did see. One side was a wall with a stream running right up against the wall. In many places the stream had cut way back into the wall. On the other side of the valley was a gradually sloping grass and tree filled ramp up to the level of the top of the wall. It was like God had dug a slopping ramp a half mile long down to a place where He just quit when He hit stone. Don't get me wrong, He coulda smacked the rock and moved it. I'm just saying what it looked like to me at the moment.

Tommy went wide up the slope into the trees. I motioned for Buck to stay behind me. All of a sudden it hit me. I didn't know what this horse would do if the shooting started. 'Hey, Lord. Please keep an eye on this horse and let me hang on. Please. Thank you, Amen.'

I rode along the stream.

A spot where the stream had been blocked a bit by rolling rocks across its width, caused a pool of fifteen feet across and two feet deep right in front of mouth of a cave. The cave looked like it was natural. The top of the dam lined up with the cave and on my side of the stream, 50 feet or so, was a pile of smaller rock that looked different than the rock the cave was in. There were no fresh tracks anywhere except for one set where Buck had come close a couple days before.

I got off the horse, dropped the reins, and walked across the dam. The cave opening was natural. No sign on it of any tools, but inside the mouth ten feet, I could see a pick and a single jack standing against the wall with a couple of drill steels alongside. A wooden box just like one I had seen for blasting powder over by Amarillo, which seemed like a long time ago, leaned against the wall.

I walked up close and read the label. AJAX BLASTING POWDER. I lifted it and moved it up to the trees behind a bunch of scrub and rock with Buck's help. Actually, he grabbed it and rode up there while I walked empty handed.

Returning to the hole, I was in a quandary. That hole was dark. How far could I go in and be safe? I had no light of any kind. 'Lord, I need to see what's in there. Any ideas?' All I came up with was that small voice in the back of my head saying, 'walk.'

I did, carrying my little pointy headed hammer.

Thirty feet in it was so dark the floor was difficult to see and there were no more colors, just dark shapes and space. Running my hands up the wall on the right side and across the ceiling I came to a foot wide hole. I checked it out by running my hand along the hole toward the entrance. It ended ten feet back. Now that I was looking toward the light of the entrance I could see a bit better. At the edge of the slot in the ceiling were whitish rocks with lines in them.

I went back to the thirty foot area, took a whack at the edge of the slot with the hammer, and brought down a fair sized slab of the roof, a few pieces hit me on my hat. Bending over, I grabbed the slab and made for the entrance.

In the noon sun the whitish stone looked white as snow and the lines were a dull, rusty yellow. The rock crumbled with very little effort. The tough parts felt the hammer. Tommy came down from the trees, took one look, and said, "Gold, or my name's little Suzy Brown."

"Gold?" said I.

"Gold?" Buck said.

"Yeah, that's gold. That's the kind gold-miners love to see, cain't remember what it's called, but they love it. You can sit here with your little hammer and crumble it, separating the white quartz from the gold veins, and walk away with almost pure gold to take to town. Most banks'll give ya 90 to 95 percent of the ounce price without any further refining. Why heck, you can refine it in a forge down to dang near the pure stuff."

We all said, "Woooweee," at the same time as we stood there gawking.

Tommy looked around and found a couple of sappy pine knots. Buck got a fire going. When we put the two together I had two torches to go in the mine with. They smoked a bit, but put out a fair amount of light. Forty feet in the veins of rusty yellow got bigger and the channel in the ceiling went wider and wider. All I could think of was, 'Diane's gonna be a rich gal. This mine has enough gold showing to restock the ranch and build those line shacks she wanted.' It was just a shame that her daddy wasn't going to get to see it.

I left the mine without burning out the first torch. A dunk in the stream simmered it to out and both were put in a crack twenty feet south of the entrance so no one would see them if they happened to drop by.

We headed for the ranch house with some good news for a change.

Diane cried all the way through the meal she prepared and set before us. I said Grace and the crying started all over again. It took the time I needed to eat the steak in front of me and five biscuits for her to settle down enough to talk about it. "What would I have done without you all? I feel so good and so bad all at the same time. Cicero missing. Shorts dead. Tor hurt bad. All those gun hands dead and even that horrible Mr. Everson dead. All over gold. I wish it wasn't there. Why couldn't it be on someone else's ranch? My mother homesteaded that section just because of the water. My father always said that place was a waste because it was so far out and hard to get to. I wish he was here now." Her bawling wiped out the rest.

I went for a walk. I had a lot of questions I wanted answered. Why homestead a place that far out even with water? Who was digging the hole deeper into the wall? Who found it? "What do I do next, Lord? I really need You to tell me."

Everything seemed so done. The kidnapper/killers were all accounted for. Diane was safe. The hands remaining were trustworthy. Everybody else we knew of was buried, some rather hurriedly. I could leave whenever I wanted to.

Tommy died that night.

Tommy had the first watch. He never woke up me or Buck. I woke at the first hint of dawn and saw Buck's bunk occupied. I didn't even bother to check my boots for varmints before I kicked my feet into them. Grabbing my gun belt I whipped it around my hips and missed catching the buckle. I tried again and succeeded. The yard was empty. The house was quiet. All the horses seemed to be in the corral. Solomon looked at me like, 'What's up, Deacon?'

I found Tommy in the kitchen with a cup of coffee on his finger. The coffee was ice cold. I put the pot on the stove and added some kindling, blew on the ashes, and had a fire in a minute or so. Buck ran in, saw Tommy, and asked very quietly, "What happened?"

I told him all I knew.

Tommy's body lay on the floor just as I had found him. He had soiled himself and his face was one of agony. His back was arched backwards. The coffee that had been in the cup must have gone down his gullet because none was seen spilled on the floor except one large drop under the lip of the cup that was still hanging on his finger.

The pot on the stove boiled. I reached for a cup on the counter and handed it to Buck. He grabbed the pot and poured as I reached for another cup.

I dropped it and spun around, slapping Buck's full cup from his lips. The hot coffee splattered on both of us. My shirt caught some, but I leaned forward to give the hot coffee distance from my skin. Buck wasn't as lucky. The scalding coffee splashed on his cheek and ear before pouring off his face and down his back. He screamed like a gut shot horse. I grabbed the water bucket and doused him with half a bucket of water.

32

"Thanks, I think. What was that all about?"

"The coffee is the only way Tommy could have been poisoned."

"How do you know he was poisoned?"

"The box in the far corner of the counter. See, the one that says 'rat poison' on it."

"Oh, thank you, Deacon."

Diane walked into the kitchen with her wrong shaped robe wrapped around her and fear in her eyes. "What's all the . . ."

She saw Tommy.

"Is he dead?"

"Yes. Poison," Buck answered.

"Oh, my god."

"Ma'am. I wish you wouldn't say that unless you know God up close and personal."

"How'd he die?"

"Poison. I already told you that."

"You don't have to yell." The crying started all over again. "Damn gold." She turned and walked back to her room.

I heard the door slam.

"Let's get him out to the barn, Buck. Did you see that box on the counter at dinner?"

"No. No one puts poison on the kitchen counter." He looked around. "Do they?"

"Someone did. Far's I can see, either you or Diane put it there, cuz I know I didn't do it."

"You can count me out. I know I didn't do it either."

I just shook my head and grabbed Tommy under his arms. He was cold and stiff. Buck grabbed his feet. The barn was cool and a board across a stall became his marble slab until the grave was ready for him.

Diane was still in her room with the door shut when we returned to the house. "I'll cook, you watch," I said.

"I'm watching after I get rid of this rat poison." Buck walked out the back door. I watched him go a hundred yards from the house and slowly pour the poison out of the box onto the ground in a thin stream. The morning breeze kicked up a bit to help disperse the poison. He brought the box back and threw it in the stove.

We both watched it burn to ashes. I stirred the ashes. It was gone.

Three of us on the ranch and one of us was a killer.

Then my brain kicked in again. It wasn't me. The reason for the murder was important. Tommy knew where the gold was. Of course, so did Diane and Buck. Diane already owned the gold mine. That only left Buck, and he didn't act like a killer. He was genuinely startled and surprised when his saw Tommy on the floor. So was Diane.

Was there someone else on the ranch trying to kill us off? Why? Because that someone else knew about the gold and did not have a prayer of getting it without killing us off. That had to be it.

My head hurt as I grilled some steaks in a fry pan and burned some biscuits in the oven.

We ate it all regardless.

I told Buck I was camping out a ways tonight. I informed Diane of my decision and she just shrugged, locked her bedroom door, and yelled, "All you brave men leaving a woman at home to guard the fort. Oh well, I guess it is my ranch so it's up to me to keep it. I won't move outta this room tonight and I want everyone to know, I have a Winchester and two pistols in here. I know how to use them and I can't miss if you come through the window or the door. Goodnight." Her lamp went out.

I had done so much figuring that I was wondering if I was guilty of the murder of Tommy, by accident. We had really torn that kitchen apart a looking for all we needed to cook and serve a big meal, any one of us could have left that poison on the counter. Although, I can say I don't ever remember seeing it in the kitchen or anywhere before.

I just started riding trying to keep the moon light bright around me while I was in shadows and under cover. After a mile or so I just rode. The dog appeared beside me just sauntering along with the horse's quick walk. So here we were so deep in the mystery, but all together like we had been shortly after it began. The dog wasn't too talkative, so I just shut up and rode.

Without thinking I had ridden toward the mine and come in on the high side of the ramped valley. I set up camp near the high end of the slope and settled in for a night's sleep in peace and quiet.

Solomon's grunt woke me up. I didn't move. I didn't open my eyes. I prayed that my breathing hadn't changed any. Someone was very close to me. How did I know? I don't know, I just knew.

A foot stepped in the gravel.

Another.

A sixgun rubbing leather as it was drawn.

I rolled.

All sound stopped, but my hand was on my blood red cross engraved pistol handle.

Another step.

I rolled fast, pulling the hammer back and letting a lead slug fly toward the shadow that appeared as I opened my eyes. The shadow dropped with a grunt and intake of air a man makes when he's hurt bad.

I rolled again.

The shadow, which I couldn't see now, fired two quick shots into where I had been. All I could think was that makes two more holes in that saddle blanket.

Now I was blind due to the flash of his gun.

I heard him or her running into the woods downhill toward the mine. I waited until the moon came out from behind a cloud and my night vision began to come back. When I could make out trees and tell them from a horse, I moved downhill taking a wide sweep to the left where I remembered there was thick brush in places and lots of trees, big trees.

I turned Solomon loose as I went past him and told him to stay close unless something happened to me, like he understood me or something.

As I walked, my boots crunched everything they touched. I took them off and hung them on a couple broken off branches so I could find them later. I walked quieter, much quieter.

The sound of splashing through the stream, probably the pool, told me a lot. If there weren't two of the enemy here, the one had just gone in the mine.

Picturing the mine, I thought perhaps he had a smallish cowpony in the mine waiting for him.

Something moved off to my right. Something big. I went to ground. A fair sized pine was between my position and the big thing. I was ready to shoot when I realized it was a horse. A small cowpony. I let it walk right up to me and stood to greet it.

I knew the horse. Only one man had ever ridden it until he died. That man was Shorts. Shorts' horse had come all the way here. I might believe that he would return to the ranch, but not way out here.

I buried Shorts so I knew it wasn't him down there in the mine. There was just one other man that might have brought that horse here.

Stepping out in the open I yelled, "Cicero, come on out. I'll see ya get a fair hearing."

No reply. The horse walked to the creek, bent down and drank.

"Come on, Cicero. It's all over. You killed a lot of people, but you're done, finished, it's all over."

No sound.

"I'm coming in, Cicero."

I walked keeping the horse between me and the mine mouth. Approaching the line of sight I needed kept me drifting down stream until I stepped over the stream and walked along the wall toward the mine. Every two little steps I stopped to listen.

Nothing.

I arrived at the edge of the mine entrance. There was no way I wanted to do what I had to do. He had ridden with me. We shared the hunger of the hunt. At one point I think he even saved my life.

"Cicero," I said softly, "Come out, now. Toss your gun out first and then come out. God can forgive anything. You said you were a believer. Believe God can forgive your greed and the murders. I'll work on forgiving you and make sure you get a fair trial."

After a few moments of listening to the music of the stream, I heard, "God don't want me. I'm hurt. You hit me bad. I can't come out."

"Was it you that put the poison in the coffee?"

"Me, use poison? Of course not."

The tone of his voice made a lie of the words and many of the words I had been hearing since I first met him.

"I would have never given you the label of liar and murderer until now. I'm coming in. Put your gun on the ground, I'm comin' to get you."

"Come get me and take me out of this hole so I can die looking up at the moon."

I could hear the pain he was feeling in his voice. He was a hurting man. At least that was true. "I'm coming in."

Entering the mine, he should have been able to see me silhouetted by the light of the moon behind me. I slid into the hole and then along the left side, my back rubbing the wall and my sixgun pointed deep into the cave. "Where are you?"

"Here." A grunt and then a shot.

A line of flame come toward me and finished off my night vision again. My hand started pulling the hammer back and then the trigger until I had fired four rounds.

He screamed again.

This time I could hear death grab him and wrestle him deep down to hell where the unrepentant always go.

I went outside, started a fire, got the pine knots, lit the unused one, and returned to drag Cicero out and across the stream where I laid him out like he was in a coffin before I went back in to find a shovel at the face of the mine.

With him buried I rode back to the Rafter B, sleeping in the saddle as Solomon took me where I needed to go and the dog tagged along.

The sun came up on me lying in my blanket in the dirt behind the house. Now I could tell Diane and Buck that it was really over. Diane could get a few miners to work the mine. Within days of beginning work there, she could afford all the cows she wanted. Buck could ramrod for her, he was a capable man.

Me? I could go back to Evelyn and figure out what was next in my life of being the Deacon, a servant to the Church.

Another dream.

33

Two days later, with Solomon all packed up and another horse - one from the outlaw Lazy E crew - packed with almost nothing, I headed for Golden. The plan was to load up the pack horse with food and other supplies - I had a list - and hire a couple of hands to bring back to the ranch and work there, while I went on to Denver and the Caravan, hopefully with Evelyn if she waited. Oh, I wasn't going to marry her, but we made a good team for the Lord. I had two or three great sermons in my head that needed to be preached.

Arriving at the main street of Golden, I checked the horses into the livery down the alley from the hotel and then walked into the hotel. The lobby was busier than on the last visit. The windows had been fresh washed and the furniture was polished and waxed to shine like the sun itself. On one of those shiny pieces of furniture was a familiar face.

"Daniel, come and sit down."

"Tor, what's up with you? I left you in that little town to recuperate, not hibernate or retire here."

"Well, I'd like to tell ya right now, but it's my bed time. I am under strict Doctor's orders. If I don't live up to those orders I will be fired and the good Doctor's bill will be mine to pay." He got up stiffly and walked to the stairs with the stiffness of a very old man with all kinds of rheumatism.

"I'll meet ya here in the morning. What time?"

"Make it about eight. And, do I have a surprise for you. Sleep tight and don't let the bedbugs bite."

The desk man yelled, "We have no bed bugs in this hotel."

Tor chuckled. "See ya at eight. I'll bring the surprise."

"I can wait. I need the sleep." I turned to the desk, "Sir, a bed now or I perish."

"Boy. Take this man to room 305 and hang the 'Do Not Disturb' sign out for him. His rig is right there by the settee. Make it quick before he faints from exhaustion, Boy." The desk clerk was studying to be in a traveling show. He wasn't bad, at that.

"Yes, Sir."

It was everything I could do to keep up with the young man he called, Boy, but I made it. He did hang the sign after my gear was put on a rack inside next to the door. The lamp was turned down. I blew it out as he closed the door with, "Good night."

"Wake me at seven please and have the barber fill a tub for me."

"Yes, Sir." I heard from the hall.

The pounding on the door was deafening. "I'm coming."

"It's 7:20, Sir. I've been trying to rouse you for twenty minutes."

"I'll be down for the barber in five. I'll want a shave and a bath."

"Yes, Sir. The bath is waiting. It might be a touch cool by now."

"Get out of here. I'm coming."

I grabbed the cleanest clothes I had, the ones I had been wearing for the last week, and stomped down the stairs.

The barber was waiting with hot water, a razor, and soap.

As I finished and was getting ready to dress, he returned. "Sir, you surely cannot wear those same clothes. I had the Boy iron out the store creases in these. Your Mr. Tor has paid for them. He stated that he would be waiting in the café you two ate breakfast in last."

"Thank you." I wanted to toss him a dollar, but I was broke until I could get to the bank and get some dollars for the gold in my bags.

"Mr. Tor said for you to not worry about money."

"Thank you."

Then I thought, 'What is this guy, a mindreader?'

I dried and dressed. Brushing my hat was a waste, but I did it.

The café was a hole in the wall where an old roundup cookie held sway with a spatula and a cleaver. Tor was waiting for me at a back corner table sipping a cup of what I assumed to be coffee. I sat down with him and told the waiter, "I'll have what he's having."

Tor smiled.

The man delivered the cup and I took a testing sip. "TEA! You're drinking tea?"

"Yeah, according to this Doctor I have, it's supposed to promote healing and I need all the promoting I can get."

"How much longer before you can ride back to Denver with me?

"Don't know that I'll be going back to Denver. Sent the Marshall a note to tell him I'm probably out of the law business. Thinking about ranching with my new partner."

"New partner?" That was a surprise, but then a lot had happened since we separated not that long ago.

"Order up. I'm hungrier than a sore toothed bear."

"So what's the surprise?"

He put a dumb grin on his face, "It's comin'. Don't you be worrying none."

My mouth was full of steak and fried potatoes when Tor whispered, "Here she comes."

"She?" I turned to see who he was talking about.

Coming across the room was a stunning young woman in a wool shirt and denim trousers. Her hair was the darkest of blacks. The way she walked said 'look out here I come and I am confident.' Then her eyes focused on me. Those eyes were dark and seemed to penetrate deeply whatever they focused on. "And, who is this lovely young lady?"

"This is my new partner. She has nursed me and wants me to work her ranch with her. I asked her to marry me last night and she is supposed to answer this morning."

"Oh."

I could not take my eyes off her.

Arriving at the table triggered my manners. I stood. She stuck out her hand which I took strictly out of habit. "I'm Diane. This man here has told me all about the Deacon."

She looked at Tor, "The answer's 'yes' to your question last evening. I have already talked with the local Parson and he can do the ceremony this afternoon if that's satisfactory with you."

"Whatever you say, Dear." He tried to stand to greet her. "But, I think we outta wait."

"Sit down. You aren't ready for standing alone and walking, yet."

"How'd you get here, then?" I asked.

"Got me a fancy chair with wheels. The boy from the hotel pushes me around when Diane's not available."

"How can we have two Dianes in our lives?" I asked.

"We can't. One of them is a fake."

34

I sat down. My brain went to work with the extra pressure on it. "Diane is a fake."

"One of them is."

I looked at the strong woman still standing at the table and stood up again. Sliding her chair out, "Would you care to join us at the table and have some breakfast?"

"I would." She sat and slid herself up to the table.

I sat. "So, tell me about all this. I am, shall we say, befuddled."

"Dad had come to Golden to meet me coming back from school in Philadelphia. I got here and he wasn't here so I was waiting when Tor came into town in a spring wagon. He was shot full of holes. The man that delivered him to the doctor didn't think he was going to live much longer. My training was nursing, so the Doctor asked me to wait on him hand and foot until he was well. He's been ordering me around ever since. The gal you chased all over the country and rescued was an imposter. I am sure she was the daughter of that Lazy E owner. They've been after the ranch for a long time and Dad was getting a bit leery of their activities. We were missing cows and hands were leaving without notice. They would just come in, get their gear, and leave. My last letter from Dad said that someone was shooting up the place without really trying to hit anything. He was worried they would start shooting to kill. So, here I am. I left school and caught the next train. I had wired the Doctor here to let him know I was coming."

"Sorry about your Dad. Wish we had gotten there sooner."

She looked at Tor, "When do you want to do the wedding?"

"When I'm ready for the honeymoon."

"I am not waiting that long before I go to the ranch, cowboy. Today or six months from now. Take your pick."

"Now, of course."

I chimed in with, "I was told in Denver I could do weddings." I smiled.

"Who said that?" Tor asked.

"Evelyn."

"Who's Evelyn?"

"My singer."

"We'll use the Parson," Diane ended the conversation.

We talked a bit longer while we finished breakfast. I left to get a spring wagon from the livery along with a couple of horses to pull it. The wrangler was very understanding and was willing to do anything for Miss Diane and her beau. "That's a right purty woman there. Women are rare enough out here and purty ones are near impossible to find. Danged if I can even find me an ugly one."

I chuckled as I drove off to the front of the hotel.

There was no wedding that day, Diane wanted to get this all cleared up before a wedding would take place.

It was three days later when we stopped on top of the rise and looked down on the ranch house. The wagon I was driving had a seat that was plumb hard and Tor was not happy with the pile of blankets and goods he was sitting and laying on during the journey. Diane was riding Solomon because, "I can't drive a wagon," she said.

I was mad. Tor was hurting. Diane was ready to spit nails at the false Diane down below.

"I will ring her neck first and then slap her silly," Diane spit out like venom.

"Diane. Hate will burn you for the rest of your life. What happened, happened. We can get things straightened out and you will have your ranch with the gold for the rest of your life."

"Don't be preaching at me, Deacon. I've heard it all before and it did nothing to keep my dad alive." There was a tone in the statement I just could not put a label on.

"Everything dies. Why should you be exempt from death in your life?"

"Don't even try to give me that religious garbage, Mr. Deacon. I have had it up to here," she waved her hand above her head.

I pointed to my heart, "You only need it in here."

"Shut up and drive." She kicked Solomon in the ribs and headed for the ranch house as fast as that tired horse would go.

I had to take it slow. Tor was hurting and whining. Not that I could blame him any.

He said, "Catch her. That woman down there will shoot her out of the saddle if she gets half a chance."

I saw Diane jump off Solomon in the middle of the ranch yard and run to the house. The front door opened and the false Diane walked out. The two met at the edge of the porch in a collision I thought was going to kill them both. I could see the fur fly from my bouncing seat as we zigged and zagged down the slope to the yard.

We got there just in time to see the false Diane catch Diane with a beautiful roundhouse swing that caught her in the left ear. Diane went down into the dirt hard.

My eyes must have bugged out. She bounced up and laid the false Diane backpedaling into the porch, where the porch edge caught the back of her calves and laid her flat on her back. Her head hit the wood with a resounding boom and bounced. She laid there still with a small pool of blood growing under her head.

Diane moved forward and rolled the unconscious one on her side and began doctoring the head wound. Within moments the false Diane looked like a war hero with a bloody bandage around her head as she sat up on the edge of the porch.

False Diane said, "Why?"

No answer.

I moved Tor into the wheeled chair on the porch and into the house. Neither of us worried about the battle on the porch.

After returning to the porch I asked, "Where's Buck. Did you kill him, too?"

False Diane looked up at me and said, "I have killed no one, ever. Buck is out checking a rumor. A passing rider said that over two hundred head of my cows are over to the west in a large hole in the lava country. Who's the tramp?"

"The real Diane who was raised on this ranch, whose mother is buried up on that rise, whose father was killed by the Lazy E, that's who," I said.

I watched. She never blinked. "So who am I, if not the Diane who was raised on this ranch, whose mother is buried on that rise, whose father was killed by outlaws that this other Diane is probably working with?"

"Beats me, lady. I have no idea. Who are you?"

"I am Diane."

Nurse Diane came through the door. "No, you are not. I am Diane and I can prove it." She turned to me. "Deacon, in the top drawer of the dresser in the room Tor is in, you will find a tintype. Bring it out here."

I did.

I looked at it as I walked out. There was no longer a doubt in my mind. I handed it to false Diane. She took one look at it and began crying. As she shook her head the ends of the bandage flapped in the breeze. "It's my mother," said nurse Diane.

"It's not true. I don't know where she found it, but she planted the tintype while she was in there. I am Diane."

I was taken aback by her anger and pain. Why would she continue to cry and fight when the picture settled it? I asked, "When was this picture taken, Diane."

"Around spring four years ago. Dad wanted her to get the picture so he could put it on his dresser. We never got around to getting a frame for it."

I looked at False Diane. "If you are you the real Diane, what do you have for proof?"

"There was never a picture of me, but there was that picture of my mother in my room under the paper in the bottom of my jewelry box, the small wooden ammunition box on my dresser."

I retrieved the box and handed it to Nurse Diane. She fumbled the latch. "It sticks." On the second try she got it open and laid out what was left of the jewelry on a small table like it was important to her, lifted the paper, and there was nothing there.

False Diane grabbed the box and shook it. Nothing fell out. "Where did it... She found it somewhere. The ones that ransacked the house stole my mother's picture. She must have found it. What am I gonna do? Now I really do have nothing, no ranch and no picture.

I looked at the paper lying on the table. There was a slight change of color over a part of the paper that was close to the size of the supposed picture. I saw the discoloration when Nurse Diane brought it out of the box and the light came through it.

I prayed, 'Lord, I need wisdom and answers here. Please show me the truth.'

An idea hit me. I looked at false Diane, "What's the terrain like to the west?"

"Mostly slow rolling hills until you get to the mountains."

I looked at the nurse, "Diane, which direction is the nearest water hole from here. Just point."

She stalled as if to think, "I don't know if it is the one over there, or over there."

False Diane said, "There are no water holes in that direction for miles." She pointed and shook her head with a smile. She knew she was right.

"How old was your dad?"

False Diane jumped in with, "Sixty-one. He married late and I took a couple of years to come along."

I asked again of the nurse, "Alright. Diane, how old was your mother and when and why did she die?"

Nurse Diane looked lost. "What is all this questions crap? I am the daughter. I've been away for a long time and now you want all these answers."

The real Diane yelled, "My mother died three years ago from some sickness that withered her away like a hot wind on green grass. She went from a healthy woman to dead in less than four weeks. I helped dad bury her. That picture was taken just three months before she died. Come to think of it, she's buried up on the hill, but her feet are under the headstone. Dad wanted it that way so the pressure wouldn't be on her head. If you look at the head stone you'll see a five pointed star that I carved in the back of the sandstone marker one day when I was up there crying."

"She spied it all out while she was here alone with the cowboy. Tramp? You're the tramp living alone with a cowboy." Nurse Diane was scared spitless.

"Dig up the coffin and see where her feet are. No one could know that except Dad and me. We were the only ones who knew that."

I slowly picked up the paper from the jewelry box. It was plain that a tintype had been in that box at one time under that very piece of paper. As I put them together everyone could see the edge lines match up.

Nurse Diane turned and walked to Solomon as I was doing the show with the paper. As I lifted my eyes from the paper, she swung onto his back and took off like a shot. I waited to let him get up to stride and called, "Solomon."

He spun on a silver dollar and gave about ninety-five cents change before returning to the hitching rail right in front of me. False Diane the nurse landed in the dirt after her flight of fifteen feet or so.

I'll give her this. She got up and started walking away from the ranch slumped in her defeat.

I went to retrieve her. There were still questions without answers.

35

After a tough couple of days we found out that Nurse Diane was really a Diane, just not the right one for the ranch. Cicero had met her on a trip to Golden when he had the gold assayed first time. He got drunk and told her everything. Cicero had told her a lot about the ranch and where to find the gold when he was whiskey blabbing and had even invited her to the ranch where she could live at the mine and he could visit her.

She liked the idea of living in a gold mine and sooner or later would most likely have gotten rid of Cicero. The gold would have then been all hers and she could get out of the area from time to time to spend a lot of money. The first thing she was going to do was buy out the saloon and dance hall she had been working in.

So when the spring wagon brought Tor in and he was talking of the Rafter B in the hotel lobby, she figured she could worm her way in. She got the doctor to recommend her to nurse Tor. It wasn't too hard to do, Tor needed a lot of nursing. She went whole hog and coddled him until he brought up the ranch and then told him her false story. He, on the other hand, was in serious pain and befuddled somewhat during his continuing recovery and never even thought of her being an imitation of the real Diane and bought her story hook, line, and sinker. All in all, Tor was so twitterpated he couldn't think.

Bottom line, the real Diane had her ranch and the Lazy E was not going to be a problem anymore. Buck was going to stay on at the Rafter B. Tor cussed, mad at himself for getting suckered in. He decided to take on the Lazy E seein's how he no longer had a job in Denver and all the owners were dead.

The question became, what's to do with a dance hall girl named Diane. The real Diane said, "I don't want her around here. She didn't hurt anyone. Instead of helping Cicero, she did come in all the way and really make a try for the place without causing more than a bruise on my head. I'm for letting her go."

I said, "I got no complaint there. Can you just forgive her and say goodbye."

"Oh, I forgive her, but I better never see her on this ranch again."

The false Diane said, "Thank you. I probably would have hurt someone if I'd pulled it off. I think it might be time for me to change a bit in my life. I could have killed and been hung for this stunt. I sincerely like the idea of someone forgiving me for something. I surely don't deserve it." She started crying, or should I say, bawling.. The tears looked real to me.

Tor was very quiet through this conversation. He sat in his wheeled chair and just looked at the ground, until, "I have an idea. It's crazy, but it's an idea. I still need some nursing. There's a ranch to build. From the sounds of your stories, Deacon, there ain't much there worth hanging on to. I ain't no saint, never have been and probably never will be. I do kinda like the stuff the Deacon tells me about this Jesus and all. I'd like to live the Christian life I promised when I was dying." He paused to look around at all of us.

"Miss Diane, you got your ranch back and I'm sorry about your Daddy. Buck's a good man and should be a great ramrod for you. Diane, the dance hall girl, you promised to nurse me back to health. I ain't there, yet. You also promised to marry me and spend the rest of your life with me. I ain't there, either." Again the pause and the look around.

A sly grin grew on his face. He coughed and hugged himself from the pain. When it was over he said, "So, here's my proposal. Deacon, you do your ceremony in front of Buck and Miss Diane as witnesses and get me and this Diane hitched." He looked at her. "If she still wants to."

She looked up startled. Through tears more like a pair of small streams, she said, "You still want me after all the lies and such. I lied to you all along. I am not a nurse. I am a dance hall floozy, with all the baggage of a dance hall floozy."

"Yes."

"Yes, what?"

"I still want you. We can start our new lives together. This Jesus fella can forgive anything, why shouldn't I?"

She sagged to the floor.

I could see that all her defenses were gone. Her heart was tearing her body apart. She shook her head a time or two, looking at Tor. "If you want me, I am yours, but I never want to hear the words 'saloon girl' again. If I marry you, you will be my only man for the rest of my life. If you marry me, I will never ask you about your yesterdays. Deal?"

"What yesterdays?" He laughed. "That means, deal, I want you for my wife."

She moved to his chair, put her head in his lap, and cried even harder. "This is so stupid, but I'm happy."

"Deacon," Tor began. "The wedding will be this afternoon. I want you to perform it. Diane and Buck, you two are our witnesses, not only to the wedding, but to the promises made just now."

Rancher Diane began to cry as she put her arm around Nurse Diane and said, "Come on. There's a dress in here just for occasions like this. It was my mother's wedding dress. It ain't much, but I'd be proud if you wore it before I do." She stuck up her crossed fingers, "I hope."

As she finished that she was looking at me.

I shook my head.

I did the wedding.

The couple left for the Lazy E an hour later using the spring wagon and towing a couple of horses.

Rancher Diane went into the house and I could smell the lunch she was fixin'.

Buck looked at me, shook his head, and went in the bunk house.

We never did find out who the "Burrrr" was that needed killing. I figure it was just a sound he made as he died.

Me, I went home to Evelyn to get my head on straight after all the killing and rescuing and just plain miracles.

If God was for me, who could stand against me. I could see me getting real proud in a short time. My thinking could turn to - 'Since I am so good, no one can stand against me.'

For the first time in my life I felt fear so deep I trembled and froze. Fortunately, I was on Solomon and he was headed for Denver with the dog right beside him.

It wasn't about the money after all.

WELL, HEY!

Did you enjoy this book?

Got a comment?

Tell Doug at

writingsailor@gmail.com

Get his other books at

www.amazon.com/author/dougball

for paperback or Kindle

www.smashwords/profile/view/DougBall

for all ebook formats

Watch for

<u>Death by Base Ball</u>

Spring of 2016

Wanna follow Doug?

www.dougball.com

Made in United States
North Haven, CT
17 May 2024

52663687R00157